beg me

M. MALONE

Beg Me by M. Malone

Published by CrushStar Romance

An Imprint of CrushStar Multimedia LLC

440 N. Barranca Ave #9016

Covina, CA 91723

www.MMaloneBooks.com

Beg Me © 2018 M. Malone

Editor: Angie Ramey

For permissions contact: CrushStar Multimedia LLC

ISBN 9781938789632 (print) | ISBN 9781938789427 (ebook)

Cover Design © CrushStar Multimedia LLC

Printed in United States of America

First Edition

contents

beg me

the confession

MILO

I LIKE TO WIN.

Well, everyone likes to win, I suppose, but most aren't willing to do what it takes to get there. To cross the finish line. To grab the brass ring. Most people want the glory without the grime it takes to work for it. But I've always been willing to get right down in the trenches and roll around in the muck to get what I want.

The key to getting ahead is understanding people and what makes them tick. And let me tell you, hubris is the downfall of many. I'm a cocky bastard, but I've earned the right. I pay attention, I do the work, and I don't make mistakes.

Which is how I've found myself at a complete loss as to how I've fucked up so completely.

I'm going to tell you the story of how I pissed off a girl, saved our company, made the bet of a lifetime, and pissed off the girl some more.

So get comfortable. Hell, grab a snack because this is going to take a while.

one

"THIS IS *NOT* HAPPENING AGAIN."

The woman who propositioned me in the dark hallway outside the bathroom squints down at my still deflated package, which, quite frankly, is not a good feeling. What man wants a woman to have to squint to see what he's working with?

Not me. And truthfully, that's never been an issue before. Some people are just blessed in the third-leg department. I'm lucky enough to be one of them.

But right now, she's squinting. Hard. Like, *searching for a needle in a haystack* hard.

What is she searching for you ask?

Not my cock. That's large and in charge and currently held snug in her tight grip. What she's searching for is what my cock is supposed to be doing right now.

That's right. She's searching for my hard-on, which apparently fled the building as soon as she got me behind closed doors.

Humiliation mixes with panic, and I take a deep breath. The last time this happened was the prior weekend on a date with a woman I met at the coffee shop. I paid for her mocha cappuccino and she responded by writing her number on the side of my cup. We went to dinner at a new restaurant near her place, and she invited me up so I could be her dessert.

It could have been the hottest thing ever if my dick hadn't decided to take a nap as soon as she took her clothes off.

Time to focus. I direct all my energy and attention to the source of my current frustration. Until recently, he's never let me down. All I have to do is figure out what's blocking him from performing. I'm here with a beautiful woman who has her D-cup breasts gloriously unrestrained and ready to pop out of her strappy little black dress at any moment.

She's ready, she's willing, and we're alone. Perfect recipe for success.

But when I look down at the soldier in question... nothing.

"Fucking hell," I mutter in disbelief.

"It's okay," she assures me, which is a nice thing to do

since in her position I'd be pissed off. Then again, she seems like a nice lady.

What was her name again?

Justine?

Jasmine?

Jessica?

"It happens to the best of us sometimes," she continues. "You're so fucking hot, I figured I'd take my shot before you left. I heard your coworkers mention you'd be leaving soon."

Under any other circumstances, the mention of my coworkers would be the ultimate buzzkill, but not today. Because dirty thoughts about one of my coworkers in particular are to blame for why I'm standing in the middle of the women's bathroom at a bar.

Mya Taylor. Rival ad executive, leading scorer in my wet dreams, and titanium ballbuster extraordinaire, aka the hottest woman I've ever met.

And she hates me.

My cock stirs at the thought of her, which should give me hope but instead is just maddening. With dawning horror, I realize my suspicions are true. The same thing happened last weekend. I couldn't get him up when I was with Brittany, but as soon as I went home and saw a work-related email from Mya, there was an instant party in my pants.

Clearly, it's not that my rooster won't crow, but he's

suddenly developed a preference for women with the ability to derail my career and make me feel completely inadequate at the same time.

For Mya.

Oh no, I think down at the offending appendage. *You do not get to react to the thought of that she-devil.*

Not that he listens to me. My cock has violated the no-imagining-Mya rule everywhere from my shower to my dreams at night. Apparently, this traitor doesn't care about my future, my career, or my sanity.

The door to the bathroom rattles and then crashes open. As if thoughts of her have summoned her directly to the source, Mya fills the doorway. Her eyes widen slightly when she takes in my naked ass pressed against the bathroom counter and the scantily clad brunette who still has my limp Judas in her hand.

Except he's not limp anymore.

As my eyes take her in, every synapse in my brain fires in delight. Mya's parents are from the Bahamas, and she has the whole *I'm a radiant and sun-kissed goddess every fucking day* thing going on. She tosses her long braid over her shoulder before glaring at me. It's as thick as rope and jet black. The millions of bangles she always wears clack mockingly as she moves.

Goddamn, the woman drives me insane.

But she also turns me on, which is evidenced by the

instant steel injection that takes me from limp noodle to solid baseball bat in less than 2.5 seconds.

"Look, it's working!" Justine-Jasmine-Jessica squeals and punctuates the statement by bouncing up and down.

Mya looks between the D cups threatening to punch me in the face and my solid ten inches. Then she glances up at me.

"Seems I'm interrupting," she murmurs. "Wouldn't want to do that."

Her words echo even after the door swings shut behind her. And my dick deflates like all the wind beneath his wings just followed her out of the room. Because that's the way he's been operating lately. He only gets hard for the one woman who takes pleasure in wounding my ego as if it's second nature.

I know she seems nice, but don't let the sweet smile fool you. She's evil and, no doubt, already thinking up some way to use this situation against me.

Then the door swings open, and Mya pokes her head back in. "Miss? I'm sorry to interrupt again. What's your name?"

"Jessica," the brunette squeaks timidly.

Mya inclines her head to the woman still holding my dick as formally as if they were meeting at a business conference.

"I thought so. Your boss is looking for you, but I can stall him another few minutes or so." Her lips curl up into a wicked grin as her eyes slide over to mine. "I'm sure it won't take much longer than that."

Then she lets the door close again, leaving the two of us alone with my rapidly softening dick and a whole hell of a lot of awkwardness.

Do you see what I mean now?

Pure. Evil.

———

DESPITE THE INTERRUPTION, Jessica is still game to continue, if you can believe that. But Mya's parting words struck the final death blow to the dick engine that couldn't. I stuff him back in my jeans and vow to get the hell out of there before I do something really stupid.

Well, more stupid than banging the bartender in the bathroom during a company-sponsored happy hour.

I follow Jessica back out into the dark hallway, and luckily, we're saved from any awkward post-not-quite-sex talk by the appearance of a big burly guy.

"Jessica? Where the fuck have you been? It's crazy out here!"

He's a large guy, taller and broader than me, but the way he's talking to her immediately puts my back up. But before I can intervene, Jessica puts her hands on her hips.

"Seriously, Mark? It's been like ninety seconds. Calm down."

When she says that, he glances at me and smirks. Okay, so much for sticking up for her. I think Jessica can take care of herself.

I mumble a quick, "See ya," and walk back down the dark hallway to the bar. It's one of those places that keeps the lights low not just for ambiance but to disguise how shitty everything looks. Several televisions hang around the room blaring a basketball game, and there are about a hundred more people crammed in here than before I snuck off to the bathroom for what should have been a quick round of fun.

There's not much fun in discovering that your equipment is out of service, so I approach the bar to settle my tab.

But before I can get there, I'm stopped by a peal of laughter coming from the corner of the bar. Mya stands with a few of our other coworkers, taking delicate sips from the beer in her right hand.

Funny, I never knew a succubus could consume human food.

"What can I get for you?"

The other bartender, a guy who looks barely old enough to serve alcohol, has a white towel slung over his shoulder and a permanent scowl on his face. Considering the crowds of people waving for his attention, I can understand why he's pissed. Jessica bailed and left him alone to deal with this.

"I'll have a beer. Whatever you have on tap."

He nods briskly and then moves on to the next person, taking orders while he's pouring. He *thunks* my beer on the bar unceremoniously before he moves on down the line.

A hand lands on my shoulder. I don't have to feign surprise at the sight of Seth Barrington, a venture capitalist who is richer than God, sitting on the bar stool next to me.

"Whoa! You made it. I never thought I'd see you sitting in a dive bar amongst the unwashed masses."

He chuckles and raises a finger and, just like everyone else in Seth's life, the bartender rushes to do his bidding. Before he can get there, Jessica steps in front of him. It's like I suddenly don't exist. Now she's only got eyes for Seth, not that I'm surprised. He's dressed in a suit that probably cost as much as my car, and the guy even smells like money. I can see the dollar signs in her eyes from here. She's fishing for a bigger catch now.

"Hello, sir. What can I do for you?" Her voice is sultry as she twirls a lock of hair around her finger and sticks her chest out.

Seth barely blinks. "Macallan 25. Neat."

"Oh, I'm so sorry. We actually don't carry that. We have Johnnie Walker."

He starts to say something else but then glances over at me. "You know what, never mind. Just water. And bring my friend another of whatever he's having, please. Thank you."

Jessica glances over at me and her smile drops slightly. "Of course. I'll be right back with those."

Once she's gone, his grin stretches so far it almost eats his face. "Dude, I could feel that tension. Is she an ex?" He frowns. "Or a not-yet ex?"

I shake my head. "She's an it-never-happened. Don't ask."

"Right. Not asking." He looks around the bar. "It's been a while since I've just... hung out."

At his words, I resolve to invite him out more often, not just when I'm trying to impress my boss. He's a good guy, and over the past year of working together, he's become more friend than client. The guy has it made but barely leaves his office. He needs to enjoy life more.

"I've been telling you to get out. You work more than anybody I know. And in the advertising world, that's saying something."

He shrugged. "Business is the same way. This is all I know. All this other stuff, talking, socializing, it might as well be a completely different culture. I feel like everyone's speaking a foreign language."

Something about the way he looks around the bar feels eerily familiar.

He's lonely.

When I first moved to DC, I was ready to take on the world, too. Then I discovered how difficult it really is to move to a new place all alone. My brother and my mom are both back in New Jersey, and even though it's not *that* far away, it's far enough. I threw myself into work, aggressively pursuing new clients for Mirage to prove to my boss that he made the right decision hiring me.

But those sixteen-hour work days come with a price tag. I know that better than anyone.

"Then let me be your translator. First, the bartender was hitting on you."

Seth chuckles lightly. "Even I caught that hint."

"Second, all of my coworkers are staring at your back because they can't believe you're real. I'm pretty sure most of them thought you were a figment of my imagination and weren't really a client."

He takes a surreptitious glance around the room before facing front again. "Center of attention. Got it."

"And third, I'm going to get you properly drunk on cheap beer and then hopefully hook you up with someone who didn't just have her hands down my pants."

Jessica shows up then with a water for Seth and another beer for me. I slide mine over to him. "Take this one to get started." I turn to Jessica. "And keep them coming."

Once she leaves, I mutter, "Somebody should get laid tonight. Even if it's not me."

MYA

I'M STANDING in the middle of a group, laughing at my friend Anya's impression of one of our coworkers. Her impressions are always spot on, and believe it or not, most of her targets are a great sport about it.

Wallace, today's unlucky pick, just rolls his eyes and finishes his beer before telling us he has to go. I wave at him before taking another swig of my beer.

Well, this is what I'm doing in reality. In my mind, I'm back in the doorway of a bar bathroom staring at the biggest dick I've ever seen.

Unfortunately, the biggest dick I've ever *seen* is attached to the biggest dick I've ever *met*.

He's handsome, I have to admit that. With coal-black hair, eyes as blue as the sky, and cheekbones that could cut glass, he's objectively beautiful. It almost makes me grumpy to admit that there's good reason women throw themselves at him.

Doesn't make me hate him any less.

"Yoo-hoo! Earth to Mya!"

I tune back into the conversation to find Anya and everyone else staring at me. Heat rushes to my cheeks. The last thing I need is for them to figure out why I'm spacing out. Anya would never let me hear the end of it, and I definitely don't want to be the subject of office gossip.

I love her, but she can't keep a secret.

To distract them, I raise my beer in the air. "Next round is on me!"

At my announcement, everyone heads back to the bar, no doubt to put more half-priced beer on my tab.

Not that I mind that much. It's a company-sponsored event, so Mirage is picking up the tab, not me personally. The whole reason we have these office happy hour events is to encourage camaraderie and make the junior staff feel like valued members of the team. Now that I'm leading my own team, this is part of the job. I smile at the thought.

I'm leading my own team at only twenty-eight years old. Ever since I moved from Maryland to Washington, DC five years ago, this has been what I've been working toward, and I'm one step closer to owning my own advertising agency one day.

The only obstacle that could possibly stand in my way is

currently sucking down cheap beer while flirting with the same bartender who just had her hands down his pants.

Milo started at the Mirage Agency a full year after I did. We weren't always openly antagonistic toward each other. In the beginning, we were almost friends. Before he was hired, I'd spent twelve months busting my ass and taking on every client, no matter how big or small, to prove that I could handle one of the agency's core accounts on my own. I've always specialized in beauty and luxury brands, and I was ready to branch out to handling a major client on my own. The Adler account, a premier jeweler, was the perfect opportunity.

I wanted that account *so badly*, and I made the mistake of confiding that desire to Milo.

And how was I rewarded? By watching him pitch an idea for the account to our boss. An idea James loved so much that he gave the account to Milo.

Ugh.

Anya steps into my field of vision, cutting off my death glare aimed at Milo's back. "So, are we going to talk about why Milo came out of the bathroom with that chick who got our beers? Right after you came out?" Then her gaze turns speculative. "Ménage?"

My jaw drops so fast it almost hurts. "Um, no thank you. I walked in right as the festivities were getting started. Or ending. I honestly couldn't tell."

Her eyes narrow. "Did you see *little Milo?*"

I take another sip of my beer to cover the disgruntled snort I can't hold back.

Little Milo.

Too bad it wasn't little, because that would give me more ammunition in our war. But unfortunately, no, the office playboy has a dick as big as his ego. Not that I'd ever tell him that. The ego in question needs no stroking, believe me.

"I didn't see anything," I lie. "Besides, it's not like I'd want to subject myself to seeing that anyway. It's bad enough having to see his face every day."

"Right. Of course."

Anya gives me a look that says she sees through my bullshit but isn't going to mention it. Smart call, considering her crush on our divorced boss is well known around the office.

"I guess we're also not going to talk about the fact that he's currently talking to Seth Barrington's fine ass over at the bar. How does he always get the best-looking clients?"

I roll my eyes and take another begrudging sip of my beer. It's the same one I've been nursing all night. Rule number one of office happy hours is not to actually drink a lot. Most of the junior associates haven't learned that lesson yet, but even when you're off the clock, you're still being judged. And James does pop in to these things every once in a while.

It would be just my luck that he'd choose to show up tonight while Milo is showing off his friendship with Washington, DC's own self-made Midas, Seth Barrington.

"He's just showing off in case James shows up," I reply when it becomes clear that she's not going to let this go. As expected, the mention of our boss shifts her focus completely.

Anya pulls the bottom of her silk blouse down slightly. "Did James mention that he'd be stopping by? He hasn't come to happy hour in ages."

"No, he didn't say anything to me. But who knows if he said anything to Golden Boy over there?"

"He's probably still stressing over that new client."

My ears perk up. Since Anya works directly for James, she always has the scoop on what's coming down the pipeline. Technically, she's not supposed to talk about it, but for someone who loves gossip as much as she does, that's more like a recommendation than a rule.

"New client? Anything I'd be interested in?"

She purses her lips. "James will kill me if this gets out, but it's definitely something you'd be interested in. All I can say is that all the wedding research you did last year might come in handy now."

At the mention of my ex, all the beer in my stomach curdles. Thankfully, I've always been discreet around the office, so most of my coworkers didn't even know I was engaged. It made it easier to come back to work the day after my fiancé told me that settling down with me felt too much like "settling."

Asshole.

"That's all you can tell me? I'm not sure how my old Pinterest boards are going to come in handy to woo a client."

Anya wants to tell me. I can see it in her eyes and by the way her mouth is one thin line, like she's physically holding her lips closed so she doesn't spill. But we're friends, and I don't want her to get into trouble, so I shrug.

"Okay, I will just have to trust you. Maybe some good will come from my fiancé dumping me after all."

She squeezes my arm. "It will. This is perfect for you, Mya. You're going to nail this one. Milo won't know what hit him."

three

MILO

I WAKE UP WITH A HANGOVER.

Apparently the universe decided that not getting laid wasn't punishment enough, so I go for a quick three-mile run downstairs in my building's gym and then jump in a cold shower. After a little pep talk, I'm ready to start my day and get back on track doing what I do best.

Winning.

Look, I'm good at almost everything. There's no point in being overly modest. It is what it is.

As I look in the full-length mirror on the back of my closet door, my reflection is like a work of art, every detail curated to exude the image I've crafted over the years. At thirty-one, I'm an executive on the fast track, but I haven't forgotten where I come from.

My mom was a single parent. My dad split when I was

so young I barely remember him, and we haven't seen him since. I saw how hard my mom worked to keep things together so my brother and I didn't suffer. Most of my clothes were hand-me-downs from my cousins, and there were multiple occasions when our lights were turned off or we had to move because we couldn't afford the rent anymore.

But as I pull on a steel-gray Tom Ford jacket and pair it with a dove-gray silk tie, I must admit that where I started and where I've landed are worlds apart.

That's why I can't allow my recent string of bad luck to get me down. I've had a few bad dates.

Not that I consider the dicktastrophe at the bar a date.

Whatever the case, I'm going to shake off the bad juju I've accumulated and get back to making deals and climbing the corporate ladder. I can't afford to make any mistakes at work, not with Mya nipping at my heels. Especially with the current rumors flying around the office. If they're true, then this is not the time to slack off.

The ride down to the first floor of my building passes quickly. Luckily, no one else is on their way out this early, so I don't have to suffer through polite conversation with any of my neighbors. By the time I reach the parking level, it's exactly 6:05 a.m.

Right on time.

My usual spot is open, so it's less than twenty minutes

after leaving my building that I'm entering the elevator at the Madison building where the Mirage Agency has its East Coast office. As I hit the button for the tenth floor, a woman enters and gives me a slow look from head to toe. She gets off on five and then gives me a little wave over her shoulder as she exits.

Yeah, I know I look good.

Here's the thing, looks are subjective and blah, blah, blah, but there's no use pretending some of us don't have an advantage.

Do women stop and do a double take when they see me? *Yes.*

Has pussy always been readily available? *Also yes.*

So if I pretended my looks have had nothing to do with my success, I'd be the worst sort of hypocrite. But the main thing that has pushed me to where I am today—wealthy, a top executive at a major ad agency and living my best life—is confidence. I've got it in spades.

You could say I have balls of steel.

No, balls of *titanium.*

The only thing that throws me off my game is—

"Good morning, Miss Taylor."

Mya pauses in the middle of the hallway and then turns slowly. Her cinnamon-brown eyes narrow slightly as if looking for the ulterior motive in my words.

"Milo. You're here early." She looks annoyed, and I realize my hunch was right. I guess she's heard the rumors, too. She's been coming in earlier and earlier trying to beat me into the office.

Yeah, good luck with that.

I've had insomnia for years. It's no hardship to come in early when you never went to sleep.

"I'm always here early. Haven't seen you in before sunrise too often though." I chuckle at the sparks in her eyes. Damn, if looks could kill she'd have me on a spit roasting over a fire by now. "You must really want that partnership, huh?"

As I walk down the hall toward my office, I hear the shuffle of Mya's feet as she jogs after me. "What does *that* mean?"

In my office, I set my briefcase next to my desk and hit the mouse to wake up my computer. Mya leans against the doorframe.

"You haven't heard?"

She crosses her arms. "Spit it out, Hamilton. Did James actually say he's taking on a partner, or is this just the millionth rumor since Elizabeth left?"

The owner of the Mirage Agency, James Lawson, has been running things alone since buying out his former partner, and former wife, Elizabeth. We all assumed he'd never consider taking on another partner. Which was disappointing because I've loved working here but knew I'd have to eventually move on as my career progressed.

But then last week, he let it slip in one of our meetings that he's been thinking of expanding and it would require a change in management.

Which of course was when I started formulating my plans.

"Not in so many words. But he did say that he wants to expand beyond the coasts. DC and LA are great, of course, but he wants Mirage to be able to compete on a national level. Which means offices in New York, Seattle, Miami, and possibly Houston to start. He'd need to have partners to handle that kind of workload, right?"

Mya's mouth falls open, fueling my usual dirty fantasies of what those lush lips can do. But before I can say something guaranteed to put the fire back in those begging brown eyes, the man in question appears in the hall behind her.

"Change of plans. I've moved the weekly status meeting to first thing today. I have a last-minute call I need to take this afternoon."

I nod at James to let him know I'll be ready. Once he leaves, Mya turns to face me again, her eyes shooting daggers.

"That partnership is mine. I've been here longer,

worked harder and been more loyal than any other associate here."

I grin. She's feeling the heat of a little competition already, huh?

My smile seems to only annoy her further, which of course gives me great incentive to keep doing it. If she only knew how much enjoyment I get watching her cheeks flush and those perfectly shaped breasts bounce behind her conservative blouses when she's pissed.

"Stop smiling, Hamilton. I'm serious. This promotion will not be just one more thing you steal from me." Then she turns on one skinny stiletto heel and twitches off.

———

MYA'S ACCUSATION is still ringing in my head hours later. What the hell does she think I stole from her?

"So, I have this idea. I think it could be even better than what we've come up with so far."

The squeaky voice of Wallace Burns assaults my ears from the right. Our team meeting just concluded, and I figured for once I'd be able to get out of there in under an hour. But... best laid plans and all that.

James glances at me briefly before nodding at Wallace. The Mirage Agency takes a team approach, which means that junior associates are assigned to the team of a senior marketing associate. Wallace is my newest team member. We encourage open communication from the lowest marketing associate to the highest executive.

Which is a great idea... in theory.

"So, I was thinking we could show the car hauling a bus. You know, to show its power. It has," Wallace glances down at his notes, "366 horsepower. That's a lot for a hybrid. We should showcase that by having it haul things through a forest or something."

"A forest?" James echoes lightly.

"Yeah. The Luxiva is going to be the most powerful yet environmentally friendly hybrid yet. I figured we could symbolize that with the forest."

Someone down the table coughs nervously. I roll my eyes. Mya's lips curl up briefly into a smile before she takes a sip of her coffee.

James gathers the files on the table in front of him. "Great initiative, Wallace. That's exactly the kind of excitement we like to see from our junior associates. We've got a winning proposal here to present to the Luxiva brand next week, but keep up the enthusiasm."

Everyone in the room takes his bullshit pat on the back for the dismissal it is, and soon the room is a flurry of movement as several bodies stand, stretch, collect coffee cups, and in general get the hell out of there.

Meanwhile I'm still thinking, *I stole something from her?*

In the hall, Wallace says, "I should've run that idea by you first, huh?"

No shit, Sherlock.

"That would have been wise."

Wallace sighs. "James probably thinks I'm an idiot now."

For sure.

"We all made our mistakes coming up."

As we approach my office, Wallace lets out a melodramatic sigh. "Can you tell me where I'm going wrong? I keep trying to come up with ideas that are different, but nothing works out."

He pushes past me and into my office without waiting for an invitation.

I look longingly down the hall toward the break room. If we're going to have a come-to-Jesus moment, couldn't we at least do it over coffee?

But the earnest look on his face touches whatever's left of my cold, dead heart, and I take a seat behind my desk.

"Let me let you in on a little secret, Wally."

He shifts uncomfortably. "Um, it's Wallace actually."

"That's a lot of name. Look, kid, people don't want different no matter what they say. Kind of like when women claim they don't care how tall a guy is or if his cock is small."

Wallace covers his crotch while nodding ruefully.

Jesus.

I don't even want to know what subconscious memory triggered that reflex.

"Your idea was the perfect example. No one dropping a hundred grand on a Luxiva gives a shit if it's environmentally friendly or can haul a bus. These are the type of people who'd buy the rainforest for their New Year's Eve party before investing money to save it."

After an awkward pause, Wallace asks, "So what do I do?"

"Remember that people want the same things they've always wanted. Luxury, power, sex. Not what they claim to want. Because most people are hypocrites."

Slow clapping interrupts.

We both turn to see Mya standing in the doorway to my office. She raises her eyebrows. "Gems of wisdom from our resident hedonist."

"Nothing wrong with pleasure, Miss Taylor. Isn't that what the luxury division of Mirage is all about?"

Mya ignores me and looks at Wallace. "Let me know if you ever decide to switch management teams, Ace. We could use a guy like you with a good heart. Or you know, a heart period."

I stand and clap the petrified-looking younger man on

the shoulder. "That's what I'll call you. Ace! Best slogan you've come up with all season, Miss Taylor."

A knock on the door interrupts. Anya, the office manager, is holding a huge bouquet of flowers. "Delivery for you, Mya. Should I put it in your office with the others?"

"Oh yes. Thank you!" Mya leaves, closing the door slightly behind her.

"I guess her boyfriend is still in the dog house," Wallace mumbles as he approaches the door.

My hand hits the wood harder than I intend and the door slams closed before he can leave. Wallace jumps back in surprise.

"Sorry, kid. What did you say about the dog house?"

I'm way more interested than I should be in the details of Miss Taylor's perfect life, but there's no denying my curiosity.

Wallace stares at me with eyes as wide as saucers. "N-Nothing. It's just that Mr. Carter has sent flowers for three days in a row now."

"I thought they broke up?"

Now Wallace is looking at me like I'm the green rookie. "They did. No guy is that romantic unless he's in trouble. I heard he cheated on her. But maybe that's just a rumor because I also heard she cheated on him."

All I can think is, *no fucking way.*

My instinctive leap to her defense is surprising. There

are very few women who earn the benefit of the doubt from me. Guys get such a bad rap for chasing tail, but women are even worse. They're just impressed by different things. Instead of tits and ass, they want power and position.

My college sweetheart, Tessa, taught me that lesson well. She was my first love, and damn did I fall hard. Until I caught her banging one of her professors in his office. Karma usually comes around in the end, though.

He didn't even give her a good grade.

"Mya wouldn't do that," I interrupt.

Wallace looks taken aback by my defense of my sworn enemy. His speculative look is making me uncomfortable, so I laugh it off.

"What? She's a man-eater and evil to the core, but she's honest. She'll at least warn you before she turns your testicles into her earrings."

He winces at that. "Well, anyway. The flowers probably mean he's trying to get her back."

I have to concede to his wisdom since I have no experience with trying to get a woman to stay. Usually, I'm trying to convince them to leave without making a scene.

"Right. Thank you, Wallace. You've been very helpful. Send me another idea for the Luxiva campaign, and I promise I'll take a look at it."

He pumps his fist in the air once and then coughs,

visibly reigning in his excitement. "Yes, sir. I'll start on it now."

He leaves with a visible spring in his step.

I barely notice because my eyes are glued to the exploding bouquet of flowers that is visible on Mya's desk down the hall. At this angle, I can't see what she's doing, but that damn bouquet is practically taking over the room. For some reason, I can't stop thinking about the rumor Wallace mentioned.

Who the fuck would cheat on a woman like Mya?

I think of some of the scathing comments she's made over the past year, but in fairness, I have to admit that I'm the only one who seems to provoke this evil side of her. Everyone else describes her as smart, focused, and fair. She's the type who'd work a long day but then take one of the interns out for drinks to celebrate their birthday, not the type to cheat on a guy and break his heart.

Which leads me back to the first theory that her boyfriend was the cheater.

Now he's sending her bouquets so big they need their own zip code. I glare at the flowers one more time before closing my office door.

If Mya is distracted by her boyfriend woes, that will make it easier for me to win this account. And I do love to win.

That's the only reason I care.

Obviously.

four

MYA

USUALLY, I have time to get a cup of coffee and check my emails before I get started for the day, but as soon as I arrive, Anya tells me an emergency meeting is taking place first thing. Immediately, I'm worried.

Did something happen with one of my accounts?

But when I get to the conference room, I notice that Kevin Barnett, team lead for the technology division, is there too, along with several others.

That makes me feel a *little* bit better.

I take a seat at the conference table next to Cole Fitzgerald, the company's public relations executive. "If you're here, the shit must have hit the fan with one of our accounts. What is it this time, sexual harassment or corporate malpractice?"

Cole shrugs, looking bewildered. "Honestly I have no

idea what's going on. I didn't call this meeting. This was arranged by the big boss himself."

I look around the table, trying not to be obvious. Kevin is across from me reading something on his phone. At the end of the table, the firm's lawyer, Ethan Westbrooke, is reading a thick document, and every few moments he stops to write furiously in the margins of the paper. Ethan is outside counsel, so James must have called him in.

"Whatever it is must be a big deal if we've all been summoned."

I note with satisfaction that Milo wasn't invited. I hope it's a new account. Since Milo has the highest number of clients, it would make sense for James to assign it to either Kevin or me.

Then the door opens and Milo saunters in. When he notices me, a smile tugs at his lips and he takes the seat right across the table.

"Great," I mutter softly.

Cole glances over. "What's wrong?" he asks before taking a sip from the small paper cup of coffee on the table in front of him.

"How long do you get in jail for murder?"

He chokes slightly and puts his coffee cup down. "A long time. A very long time."

"What if it looks like an accident?"

His lips twitch. "Not sure who has done something to

warrant an accidental homicide, but maybe I don't want to know. However, in my official capacity as head of public relations, I would have to advise against it."

"What if the guy is an asshole and no one would miss him anyway?"

"Well, why didn't you say so? That's a totally different story, of course."

Just then, James enters the room and we all snap to attention. His hair has been almost white the entire time I've known him, despite the fact that he's not even forty years old. He has a sexy Anderson Cooper kind of vibe going on, but our boss is definitely high strung.

Now is no exception, and his eyes shine with a maniacal glee as he plunks down a stack of folders on the table before he sits.

"Ladies and gentlemen, sorry for the late notice on this meeting, but I have a major announcement to make." He pauses, and everyone glances around at each other. It's not like James to grandstand or make a big production, so everyone knows it must be a big deal. "We've been asked to pitch to Lavin Couture next week."

At his words, Kevin drops his phone on the table. Milo sits up a little straighter. I glance over at Cole, and he looks stunned as well. Even he knows the significance of this.

Lavin Couture has been the darling of the fashion world for the past few years, partially because of the media's fascination with the company's namesake. Andre Lavin is a descendant of Italian royalty, blindingly photogenic, and the closest thing to our generation's Versace. People aren't just obsessed with his designs, they're obsessed with his life.

Landing a client like this would not only put Mirage on the map, it would guarantee us all job security.

"The reason I moved our weekly meeting yesterday was because I had a call with the head of design for Lavin Couture yesterday afternoon."

He pauses and waits for the excited murmurs to wane before continuing.

"Mr. Lavin has offered to send his private jet to transport us to Vegas where he's currently meeting with potential investors for his next brand launch. We'll be taking three junior associates with us. I'll allow the team leads to choose. It goes without saying that this is the biggest deal Mirage has ever lobbied for, and I expect all hands on deck this week. I know I can count on you all to continue doing exceptional work."

My eyes meet Milo's across the table. In the span of a heartbeat, a message of understanding passes between us. It's on.

He may have beaten me to the Adler account, but I'm going to be the one who locks in this partnership.

———

WHEN I GET HOME, my roommate looks up from her perch on the couch. Her face betrays her surprise. I don't even get my key out of the door before she starts on me.

"Oh my god, Oreo. Call the cops. We have an intruder!" Ariana whispers dramatically to the black-and-white Pomeranian in her lap. Oreo jumps up when she sees me and gives a single, joyful bark.

"Har, har." I ignore her as I set my messenger bag by the door and slip my heels off. It feels fantastic to release my toes into the wild after having them crammed into those narrow, pointy shoes all day. The price we pay for fashion.

"Seriously, Oreo. There's no way this can be Mya, our roommate. Because we normally only see her on Sundays. Every other day she gets in so late that any sane person is already in bed watching Netflix."

I saunter into the kitchen and snag a piece of pizza from the open box on the counter. "Maybe I'm taking your advice. Did you ever think of that? I'm trying to live a little, get off work early, hang out. All the normal things I usually don't have time for."

Ariana gets up and scrutinizes me before grabbing a piece of pizza for herself. "So, you just decided to knock off work early? Was it happy hour or something?"

"No, we had the office happy hour a few days ago. I did attend, by the way. You know James likes for us to talk to the junior associates. I put in my appearance, had a beer, and then went back to the office. But tonight, I decided to take off on time. We're pitching a major client next week, so this might be my last chance to relax for a while."

Ariana chews thoughtfully. "Happy hour, huh?"

"Is that all you heard?" I finish my slice of pizza and then kneel down to give Oreo a scratch. She gives my chin a lick before continuing to sniff the floor around my feet. Apparently, I'm not that interesting since I've already finished my pizza.

"Yes. Was he there?"

"The entire office was there." I ignore her searching look and walk over to the refrigerator for a soda.

When I close the door, she's standing right behind it. I almost drop the can of soda I'm holding. It's also the first time I get the full effect of her outfit. She's wearing a blue T-shirt that reads, *I don't trust electrons, they never do anything positive,* coupled with a pair of paint-splattered jeans.

"Redecorating? Again?"

Ari is obsessed with creating the perfect environment and repaints her room at least once per year. Yeah, I've kissed any hope of getting our security deposit back goodbye.

"Don't try to change the subject. Painting my room isn't

nearly as interesting as whether your hot-as-fuck coworker was at happy hour."

She follows me as I walk back around the kitchen counter and take a seat on the couch. I close my eyes and enjoy being off my feet, but when I open my eyes again, Ari is standing right next to me with her arms crossed. Ever since she saw Crazy Eyes on the show *Orange is the New Black*, whenever she wants me to cave, she stares at me. It works every time. Her hazel eyes have the ability to be insanely gorgeous but also really intense.

Like serial killer intense.

"Okay fine, he was there! Now can you please stop staring at me with that creepy look?" It's almost ridiculous how quickly she can break me down when I'm trying to play it cool, but we've been roommates and friends ever since I came to DC. Not many people know me as well as she does.

"I'm starting to wish I'd never told you about him," I grumble, knowing that she won't take offense.

Sure enough, she just laughs. "Yeah, right. Who else would have listened to you gushing about your dreamy new coworker back when he was first hired? That was all you talked about for months until... well, you know."

"Yeah. Until I found out he was a backstabbing jerk. Thanks for the reminder."

Ari grins. "What are friends for?"

Since we're already on the topic, I might as well unload

my latest problems. Most of my old friends from college are already married, and the only things they want to talk about these days are babies and when I think I'll take the plunge and get married, too.

I don't begrudge their happiness at all, but it's difficult to find someone who can relate to the things going on in my life anymore.

My mom always used to say that some friends are in our lives only for a season and I shouldn't try to hold on too tightly. When their time passes, they fade away to be replaced by new connections. At the time, it made me sad to think of letting go of some of the friendships that got me through college and my first jobs, but over the years, I've seen the wisdom in her advice. Ari is probably the only one who'd understand the significance of my upcoming trip.

"A major client is flying us to Vegas next week to meet with him. It's a big deal. I want this account, Ari."

"You've been talking about wanting to prove your chops to your boss, so this is your chance, right?" Her eyes gleam, and she rubs her hands together in anticipation.

She takes up her former spot on the couch and tucks her long legs underneath her. Her honey-colored hair is tucked up in a low bun, and she's got no makeup on but somehow still looks perfect. Her mom is a former model from Sweden, and her dad is some big-shot businessman from Venezuela.

Ariana is the perfect blend of them both, glamorously beautiful with the mind of a cutthroat capitalist.

Men never see her coming.

"Absolutely. This is exactly the kind of opportunity I've been waiting for. I'm going to show James everything I'm capable of and why I'm the perfect person to lead this account."

"Sounds good. So why don't you look more excited about this?"

"Because Milo is going, too. Which means I have to be on my A game, otherwise he'll steal this account, too."

She's nodding along with every word. "You know what I think? You two need to bone."

My mouth drops open, but she's not done.

"Yup. That's what needs to happen. All this animosity and tension could be solved with some boom-boom. A little bit of banging. A little bit of bam-bam in the ham."

Despite trying not to, I have tears in my eyes from laughing. "Bam-bam in the ham? That's a new one."

Ari shrugs prettily. "There's more where that came from. But seriously, you haven't been laid in forever. And no offense to Will, but with that giant stick up his ass, there's no way he was laying the pipe right. Girl, you need to get some."

I ignore her comment about Will, because let's face it,

she's totally right. "Milo and I are not boning or doing whatever with ham that you just said."

"Bam-bam in the ham," she repeats helpfully.

"Whatever." I draw my hand across my neck in a cutting motion. "Besides, I'm not into casual sex."

"Don't knock it till you try it," she drawls. "Sometimes a girl just needs to get the cobwebs out. You know, a bit of spring cleaning. As long as it's on your terms, then I say go for it."

"That's never happening. We hate each other. You know this."

"Mmm, hmm. Okay, it was just a suggestion." Her eyes drift back to the TV as her fingers continue to stroke Oreo's fur leisurely.

I want to just dismiss it as the usual Ariana nonsense, but her suggestion has taken root. Can I really pretend I didn't wake up the morning after happy hour dripping with sweat after an intense sex dream about Milo?

That doesn't really count, I rationalize. *I was sleeping. I have no control over that.*

Besides, what I saw in that bathroom didn't even look like it could be real, so anyone would be intrigued, right? What red-blooded, heterosexual woman wouldn't have lustful thoughts after seeing a handsome man with a billy club in his trousers?

But you're not just anyone. You're someone who knows

Milo and talks to him. It's not the same thing as having sex dreams about a celebrity or something.

All the internal back and forth is overwhelming. Suddenly it's like I can't hold it back anymore.

"I saw his dick!"

I clap my hand over my mouth, but it's too late. My tongue has been unleashed and it won't stop until I let it all out.

Ariana's mouth drops open. "Mya Taylor. You bitch! You saw his anaconda? When was this and why haven't you told me?"

"He was in the bathroom with some chick at happy hour, and *what was I supposed to do?* I just pretended that I didn't see anything, but the whole time, I was pissed."

Ari blinks. "You were pissed."

It's almost like she didn't hear a word I just said. "Of course, I was pissed. His dick was in her hand!"

Ari bites her lip. "And... you wanted it in *your* hand?"

"Yes! Wait, what? No. I didn't want it in *my* hand."

"In your *mouth*, then. I can understand that. I mean, I've seen the guy."

I put my fingers to my temple and massage the headache blooming right behind my eyes. "Kind of missing the point here, babe."

She looks amused. "Am I? Because I'm starting to think I'm the only one around here paying attention."

"Paying attention to what? Please enlighten me how my coworker picking up chicks in some gross bar bathroom has any relevance to my life."

Ariana pantomimes putting on a pair of glasses.

Oh god, here comes Mistress Ana.

Whenever she wants to lecture me on something she thinks is for my own good, she morphs into this parody of what she thinks a college professor looks like. Mind you, Ari looks more like a dominatrix type of Mistress than a college professor, but she doesn't care. And invariably I end up laughing my ass off, so I don't even mind that she's butting into my business.

"First, this is relevant because it upset you. Don't bother denying it because I can tell. You have no poker face whatsoever."

I want to object, but years of experience have taught me that what she says is true. Honesty is the best policy, not just because it's the right thing to do but also because I can't pull off anything else.

She holds up two fingers. "Second, it's important because it was unprofessional, and men shouldn't be able to get away with doing this shit. Can you imagine if a woman tried that at a work event?"

I'm nodding along now, because what she's saying is echoing everything that I was thinking earlier. Here I am busting my ass, doing everything I can to prove to James that

I'm competent, and my biggest competitor is getting laid at a company event. What the hell?

"And third, and most importantly," Ari continues, "is that you wish it had been you."

Before I can respond with what could have been a well thought-out, reasonable rebuttal, Mistress Ana levels me with the craziest pair of crazy eyes. "No poker face, remember."

I huff, but I let it go.

Honesty is seriously overrated.

five

MYA

I CAN DO THIS. I can do anything I put my mind to.

I am strong.

I am brave.

I repeat the words softly, hoping repetition really is the key. For the past week, the atmosphere at Mirage has been focused on one thing and one thing only.

The Vegas meeting.

We've all been working longer hours, doing research on Lavin Couture's last five collections and preparing example dossiers of our work on other fashion brands.

It's been exciting, and I'm thrilled to have this opportunity. I will not allow something like a slight fear of flying to ruin this for me, so I buckle my seatbelt and close my eyes all the way through takeoff. There's a slight bump as the wheels come up, and I let out a small squeak.

Oh, screw being brave.

My fist clenches in a death grip around the plastic cow that is the only thing standing between me and a complete nervous breakdown in the middle of this airplane.

Not that these are bad accommodations for a first-time trip to the loony bin. I've never been on a private plane before, but I can't imagine anything more luxurious than this. The seats are covered in dove-gray leather and the carpet on the floor is plusher than what's in my apartment. Gleaming gold accents adorn the armrests and the trim overhead.

Andre Lavin has the same impeccable taste in personal aviation as he does in everything else.

Unfortunately, it's all wasted on me. It's my first time flying like a rock star, and I'm two seconds away from curling up in the fetal position in the middle of the aisle.

A toothy flight attendant leans down to offer me a drink, but honestly, I'm afraid to even pry my lips apart to turn it down. So I give a tense nod, and she continues on her merry way down the aisle, offering drinks to everyone as if we aren't all in danger of plunging thousands of feet to a fiery death. I squeeze my eyes shut and start counting.

Breathe, Mya.

"Nervous flyer, huh?"

My eyes pop open at the deep baritone in my ear. Milo

has switched seats with Wallace and is now entirely too close for comfort. The last thing I need is my competition seeing my weakness.

"What makes you say that?" I'm going for nonchalant, but my voice sounds an octave higher than usual.

Milo inclines his head toward my lap. "The death grip you have on Miss Moo there."

It takes some effort, but I manage to loosen my fingers so I can show him. "This is Chelsea, the stress cow. Lots of people use them."

His eyes dance with amusement. "I don't see anyone else squeezing the life out of a plastic farm animal, do you?"

I sit up straighter, ready to let him have it, but just then the plane hits a pocket of turbulence. My stomach feels like it's now in my esophagus.

"OH MY FUCKING GOD! THIS PLANE IS GOING DOWN."

This comes out way louder than I would have hoped. Milo chuckles under his breath as everyone turns around to stare at us. After a few moments, they finally turn around, but James raises his eyebrows as if to say, *Are you okay?*

I wave and force a smile so he won't worry. When he finally looks away, the breath I've been holding releases in a gasp.

"I'll be lucky if I still have a job by the time this trip is over," I mutter under my breath. Obviously not quietly enough, because Milo laughs again.

"Imagine that. Spent your entire life on the straight and narrow and it all ends on a private plane sitting next to the devil himself."

When I glare at him, he shrugs in that nonchalant and completely hot way that totally does *not* get my panties wet.

"Just saying. I'm a big fan of irony. It just proves what I've always known."

"And what is that, oh wise one?"

"That the universe fucks us all in the end."

Dirty words coming from his mouth should not be so arousing. Especially when he's completely right about me. Not that I'll ever tell him that.

"Well, the joke is on you. You're assuming I've spent my entire life on the straight and narrow. I could have been a real bitch in my past. Maybe this flight from hell is my karma for deeds done wrong."

"Maybe," he concedes with that infuriating smirk that means he actually believes the total opposite.

"You think you know so much about me. You think I'm just this boring workaholic who goes home at night and curls up with a million cats. Admit it."

His eyes focus on me then, like two electric blue lasers. "No, I don't think that at all. But it sounds like someone else has made you believe that's true."

My last argument with William rolls through my head like a movie on repeat. Our relationship was never perfect, not even when things were new and interesting. But I'm not the kind of woman who looks for perfection anyway. I don't care about socks left on the bathroom floor or who took the trash out last. All I've ever wanted is someone who gets me.

Milo is watching me again, this time with something that looks suspiciously like pity in his eyes. He's intuitive; I'll give him that. But damn him for using that on me.

"I heard about your breakup. Sorry. That sucks."

I look out the window at the clouds passing by. Normally I don't do this. Looking at clouds from this angle just reminds me of where I am, in a tin can hurtling through the sky. But contemplating the likelihood of total engine failure is preferable right now to Milo Hamilton looking at me with pity.

"Thank you, but I'm fine. All I want is to focus on why we're flying to Las Vegas in the first place. To impress this client and snag the hottest ad account in the country right now."

Milo nods. "I'm not sure if James even went home last night. He was in the office early doing research."

I'm not surprised by that at all. Andre Lavin is the preferred designer of all of Hollywood's leading men. Although he's known for menswear, after designing both the bridal tuxedo and the wedding dress for Hollywood's reigning power couple, he was rumored to be launching an exclusive bridal line. This account could catapult the Mirage Agency into the upper echelon of advertising overnight.

If James is looking for a partner, whoever locks down this account is on the fast track.

"Let me guess, so were you?"

His tight smile confirms it. Milo hates to lose, and no doubt he was in the office almost as long as James. But he might as well get ready because I'm going to be the one to lock this account down.

"I wanted to talk to you about something," Milo leans closer. "What did you mean when you said I stole an account from you?"

My blood freezes in my veins. Had I said that? My thoughts race back to that day when he'd first told me about the partnership. Clearly I hadn't been thinking straight. I'd just been so excited.

Over the past few years, I've worked on some extraordinary campaigns. I put my heart and soul into each one, and I know I've done great work for Mirage. But so far, most of the accounts have been mid-level, and doing great work on them isn't enough to show James that I have what it takes to be promoted. I've been waiting for the type of project that would really let me show off what I can do.

This is it. Lavin Bridal is what I've been waiting for.

So that day in Milo's office, my head had been swimming with visions of the future. That's the only explanation I have for why I'd tell my nemesis that he'd ever gotten a leg up on me.

"I'm not sure what you mean. You must have misunderstood."

Milo narrows his eyes, and a beat passes in tense silence. Then he smiles, showing both rows of teeth.

Like a barracuda.

"Okay, if you want to play it that way, fine. But I don't poach accounts, and when I convince Andre Lavin to sign on the dotted line, I want it known that I did it fair and square."

"When? Hah. You really think you're going to win a bridal account? The king of one-night stands is suddenly an expert on weddings?"

I shouldn't have said that. Not only because it makes it sound like I'm keeping track of his personal life outside of the office but because it opens the door for him to bring up my own failures. Namely, being dumped six months before my own wedding. He could argue that my personal life makes me a bad candidate to pitch for this account, too.

He looks like he's thinking about taking the bait, but surprisingly his face softens. "I think that we're both willing to do whatever it takes to win this client. No matter which one of us gets to the finish line first, in the end Mirage benefits."

I look to the front of the plane where Kevin sits next to James. He's a nice guy but a bit of a suck up. He brings in clients at half the rate Milo or I do, but for some reason, James still promoted him to be a team lead.

"What if Kevin is the one to convince them to sign?"

Milo follows my gaze up front. "Seriously?"

"Okay, I admit that's unlikely."

"Look, for the next twenty-four hours, let's call a truce. We can go back to being sworn enemies when we're back in the office, but right now, we need to work together to win this. Let's lock down the account, and then we can duke it out later as to who is going to take lead."

As much as I hate to admit it, it's a fair plan. This account is a boon for the entire company, and working together, we have a better chance of convincing the Lavin team that we're the right fit.

"Agreed."

"So, truce?" He holds out his hand and we shake quickly.

The plane hits another bout of turbulence, and I squeeze the hell out of his hand. "Truce," I manage to say finally.

He carefully extricates his fingers from my death grip.

"Seriously, it's all going to work out. As long as we don't encounter any other problems, we've got this in the bag."

———

BY THE TIME we land in Vegas four hours later, I'm a quivering mess. Chelsea has been mangled between my fingers so often the plastic looks permanently deformed, and poor Wallace, who had the misfortune of sitting in front of me, heard every four-letter word in the English language.

But Milo has been strangely quiet the whole time. After his truce declaration, he put on his headphones and closed his eyes for the rest of the flight. Watching him sleep so peacefully while my heart was in my throat was extremely irritating.

It was also fascinating to watch him when he wasn't sneering at me or trying to steal my clients. When he's asleep, he almost looks... nice. Like the guy I thought he was before I found out how far he'd go to win.

Milo gets his phone out as soon as we leave the plane.

"Calling your girlfriend?" I applaud myself for keeping the disdain out of my voice when I ask.

Truce, remember?

"My mom," he replies, deadpan. "She's not a fan of planes either, so I always like to let her know when I've landed safely."

"Oh. Well, that's actually sweet."

"Considering how much she likes poetry, you'd think she'd be a bit more open to adventure. How does it go? 'For in that sleep of death what dreams may come.'"

"Is that... Shakespeare?"

He eyes me. "Why do you sound so surprised? My mother named me after John Milton. My younger brother is named Tennyson, for fuck's sake."

I pantomime zipping my lips. "I didn't say I was surprised."

But I can't deny that I'm shocked. Then I remember this is Milo. He's probably memorized sonnets to help him hit on women. "Wait, your brother is named Tennyson? Why don't I remember that?"

I met his mom and brother at last year's company Christmas party. His mom is beautiful, a discovery that's not shocking considering what Milo looks like. His younger brother is a quieter, gruffer version of Milo. He introduced himself and then didn't speak again for the rest of the night.

Milo grins. "He hates his name as much as I hate mine. He goes by Ten. Most people hear it wrong and assume it's Tom. He doesn't correct them."

Mr. Lavin arranged for a car service to pick us up, which takes us directly to the hotel. I squirm in my seat with excitement. I've always wanted to see the Bellagio. It's a beautiful hotel and makes me feel like a character in a

Hollywood heist movie. James heads straight to the front desk to get the keys to the block of rooms he reserved for us, so I take the opportunity to look around.

It's too bad we're only here for a night. I'd love to have a chance to explore more, maybe even catch a show.

"Okay, here are your keys. Most of us are on the tenth floor, but Milo you're on the twelfth. Everyone, please be on your best behavior. The Lavin team is also staying at this hotel, and you never know who might see you. Keep that in mind."

Everyone breaks off and heads for the elevators. Most of us just brought carryon bags, but Kelly, the junior associate from Kevin's team, has a huge rolling suitcase more suited to a month's vacation.

James follows my eyes and then shakes his head. "You two, I need to have a word."

Milo and I exchange glances before following him as he walks off to the side of the concierge desk. I wish I could have gotten a chance to talk to James alone before we go upstairs to get ready for dinner. I have a few ideas for the Lavin account that I wanted to run by him.

But I squash my competitive side as I remember that tonight is about securing the account more than anything.

This isn't the time to crush my competition. Milo and I have agreed to a truce, and I intend to honor it. We're going to be charming at dinner tonight and show the Lavin team all the reasons why Mirage is a perfect fit for a luxury brand. Milo's words on the plane come back.

As long as we don't encounter any other problems, we've got this in the bag.

James finally finds a space next to a rack of luggage that's private enough. He glances around before speaking.

"We have a problem."

To his credit, Milo keeps a straight face. But inside he has to be thinking the same thing I am. What now? How could there be a problem when we've just arrived? Luckily, James doesn't keep us in suspense too long. His words come out in a nervous jumble, like he's in too much of a panic to take breaths between sentences.

"Elizabeth is here. My Elizabeth," he continues as if either of us didn't know who he was talking about. "She found out about the Lavin deal somehow, and her company is talking to Lavin, too. Tonight. One of the associates she took with her when she left still talks to Anya. Apparently, they're pitching the Lavin team over drinks right before they meet with us. We might lose the job before we even get the chance to meet."

I put my hands up to catch his attention because he looks like he's on the verge of hyperventilating. "Take a breath. Let's take a step back and look at the whole situation. Andre Lavin sent his plane for us. He wouldn't have gone to all that trouble and expense if he wasn't going to listen to our pitch as well."

James's face is bright red, but he's listening to me intently. After a brief pause, he nods briskly. "That's true. He wouldn't have done that."

"So that means that no matter what Elizabeth says to him at drinks, we still have a shot at making him forget about it at dinner. And we will. Milo and I are already working on something that's going to blow him away."

"You are? Of course, you are. That's why you were talking on the plane ride." James closes his eyes, and finally, his color starts to return to normal. Or at least not one shade away from a tomato.

"I should have known you two were prepared. Anya's message didn't come through until we landed, so I think I just panicked for a moment."

Milo claps him on the shoulder and then steers him toward the elevators. "Everything is going to be fine. Why don't we go to our rooms and take a load off before the meeting? We don't want to be jetlagged and cranky later."

"Good idea." James nods and pulls his small suitcase behind him. "Are you guys coming?"

Milo hesitates. "No, you go ahead. I want to talk to the concierge. I think I forgot my toothbrush."

He gives me a look that I immediately interpret as, *We need to talk.*

"Yeah, I think I'm going to check out the gift shop before I go up," I add.

We stand together and watch as our boss gets on the first elevator going up. At least he doesn't look nearly as crazed as he did at first. Before the elevator doors close, he waves.

Then Milo turns to me. The affable smile he wore for James's benefit is gone.

"What the fuck are we going to do?"

MILO

MYA and I stand in the lobby in shock for a few minutes. Finally, she blinks and then blows out a long breath.

"No pressure, huh?"

The tension breaks and we both laugh. Jesus, as if the stakes aren't high enough already, we have to add in our boss's feud with his ex-wife. Juggling this many balls something is bound to break.

The thought gives me renewed determination to impress the Lavin team tonight. James is a good guy, if a little intense. I wasn't here when the whole thing with his wife went down, but I've seen enough of the aftermath to know how important this is.

We cannot let James down.

"I can't believe Elizabeth is here," Mya remarks as we walk toward the gift shop in the hotel.

"What's the deal with her? I wasn't around when she left, and I definitely don't want to ask James."

She shakes her head. "It happened a few months after I was hired, so this was about three years ago. Elizabeth and James started Mirage together, but then after a decade of running the business as a team, she left him for one of their clients, Gareth Whittington."

I wince. "The guy who puts on all those wild slumber parties in Hollywood?"

"That's the one. The porn king himself. James wasn't excited about taking him on as a client in the first place, but Elizabeth convinced him it was a good idea. It was a big account for us, but James was worried about all the moral implications of working with a borderline legal brand. I mean, you've heard about some of the stuff that happens at those parties, right?" Her face conveys her disgust.

Oh yeah, I've heard about them. In fact, I've attended one, not that I'll admit that to Mya. Besides, it wasn't my scene. Everyone there was either drunk, or high, and while I have nothing against wild times, I would like to at least remember what I did and who I did it with.

"Um, yeah, I've heard they can get pretty insane."

She scoffs. "Not just insane. Violent. There have been multiple court cases already about underage girls who've been drugged and abused at those parties. He was in the news just last week because some actor overdosed and no one around him even noticed until it was too late."

Oh shit.

"Okay, I didn't know all that," I admit.

"Anyway, the guy is bad news. But it turns out James shouldn't have been as worried about our image because it was his *marriage* that actually took a hit. Three months after we took on Gareth as a client, Elizabeth filed for divorce. She left and formed her own company, taking half the Mirage client list with her. She even had the balls to send him an invitation to her wedding to that guy. James still hasn't gotten over it."

I feel an instant kinship with James. We may not know each other that well, but we're part of the same brotherhood, men who once bought into the idea of true love and got kicked in the teeth. We should have membership cards.

"So, if she's the one who left, why is she so determined to get back at James?"

None of this is making sense to me. I mean, I get the *Elizabeth is a cheating bitch* part, because... obviously. Fucking a client behind your husband's back and then trying to tank the business you built together is a dick move.

What I don't get is what she wants *now*.

Mya sighs. "Because apparently part of the reason why they broke up was because he didn't like her ideas. She wanted to take the firm one direction, and he wanted to go another. I'm sure this is her way of proving to him that he was wrong."

We've reached the gift shop now, and I step back so Mya can enter before me. She has her small duffel bag thrown over her shoulder and looks like a college co-ed in her black yoga pants and long T-shirt. She makes a beeline for the right wall where all the toiletries are.

"Didn't you say you needed a toothbrush?"

I shake my head. "I just said that so James would go up without us."

"Right. Well, I actually did forget mine." She grabs a blue toothbrush and then a package of over-the-counter sleeping pills. Then after a moment of hesitation, she grabs a package of potato chips and a candy bar.

When she sees me watching, a shy smile covers her lips. "For later. Once we nail this presentation to Mr. Lavin, I'm going to need to veg out for the rest of the night. I don't travel well."

"You don't say," I drawl before grabbing a bag of chips and a package of gum for myself. "But seriously, what's the plan for tonight? Elizabeth is obviously on a mission to stick it to James, so she's going to be fighting dirty. We need to be ready."

She looks worried, and for some reason, I hate to see that look on her face.

"Hey, don't worry. I don't think Mr. Lavin is looking for

concrete plans yet. After all, he's kept everything so hush-hush about this deal that we don't even know for sure that it's a bridal line."

Mya nods. "True. But I'm getting a bad feeling about this. Like maybe Elizabeth knows something we don't."

Despite my determination to stay positive, I'm pretty sure she's right.

I DRESS CAREFULLY FOR DINNER.

Not that I don't put a lot of thought and attention into what I wear with every client, because I do, but this is Andre Lavin. The man doesn't just set trends, he starts fashion movements.

We're going to this dinner to convince him that Mirage is the best choice for his company's advertising and brand management, but make no mistake, he'll be checking us out as people, too. My hand hovers over a maroon tie before coming back to the lighter one I'm holding.

The interior of his plane was gray, so it's probably not a completely wild guess to assume he likes neutrals. Now that I think of it, most of his runway looks are monochromatic as well.

Hmmm.

Making a quick decision, I grab the gray tie. It's better to be on the conservative side until I've met him in person. My suit is already hanging in the closet, pressed and ready to go.

When I reach the lobby, the first person I see is Mya. My mouth drops open slightly. She turns, and it's like one of those scenes in a movie where time slows and birds start singing and shit.

Her dress is one of those magical drapes that probably looks like a bag when it's on the hanger, but on her body, it wraps each curve lovingly. Most of the other women roaming the lobby are wearing skirts so short you can tell whether they wear G-strings or bikinis, but Mya's dress is long enough to completely cover her knees.

Something about how she's so demurely covered up but yet rocking such obvious curves is a total turn on.

No, not a turn on. We are not turned on by a coworker.

My dick is not taking orders from my brain, as usual, so I button my jacket to give myself a little coverage. Not that it helps much, but anything is better than greeting a client with an extra arm extended for a shake.

"You're late," is the first thing out of her mouth as I approach. But I don't miss how her eyes roam up and down, taking in the custom-fitted suit and the bulge trying to bust through the seams of my pants to greet her. Her cheeks are slightly pink by the time she meets my eyes again.

If we weren't about to meet with a major potential-client, I would tease her about checking out my package, but this isn't the time to get Mya riled up. I need her on her game tonight, so I just tap my watch.

"Five minutes early, beautiful." The compliment slips out before I can question the wisdom of it, but Mya visibly blooms under the attention.

"But the Lavin Team is already here, which means we are late."

Since I've already thrown professionalism out the window, I gesture for her to spin around for me. After a slight pause she turns, giving me another glimpse of the round globes of her ass in the clinging material.

"You really are stunning, you know that?"

It comes out more intense than I meant for it to, but there's no help for it now. She's a vision and she should know it.

Mya bites her lip. "You don't think it's too short, do you?"

My eyebrows lift. "Short? It's not even showing kneecap. Half the chicks in here are flashing their Brazilians in plain view."

That gets a soft huff of laughter and the pinch in her forehead relaxes slightly. "Oh good. I didn't think so, but Will always said... well, never mind. I just like my skirts a little on the longer side."

Translation, the dipshit she was once engaged to made her feel bad about showing off her gorgeous body.

Insecure assholes are always worried about losing the woman they're with. Which should be a clue that they don't deserve the lady in question.

Before I can tell Mya exactly that, James appears at her elbow. "Mr. Lavin and his team are already seated. Luckily, Kevin and the others were early enough to greet them."

There's a subtle warning in his voice. We should have been here early and been the first ones to greet the client. Mya catches my eye and I can see that she's having the same thought.

There's no way we're letting Kevin worm his way in on this account.

Time to get our game faces on.

As we approach the table, everyone stands, and the introductions are made all around. Maybe it's because I'm watching Mr. Lavin so closely that I see how his eyes follow Mya after she shakes his hand and then walks around the table to greet the other members of his team. She knows all of their names, as do I. Then she takes a seat right next to me.

Before I can even sit down, James is already ordering a scotch from the waitress. Then I see why.

Elizabeth is sitting two tables away.

She raises her glass of wine in our direction. I turn to see James give a begrudging wave. I'm not sure if anyone else has noticed her yet, but she's already accomplished her goal.

There's no way James can focus completely on the client tonight with his ex-wife sitting right in his line of vision.

"Thank you all for traveling to meet with me. I've had this week scheduled with potential investors for months, so it's been helpful that you could come to me while I'm already in the States."

"When do you go back to Italy?" Wallace asks. "I follow you on Instagram. You guys, his page is *lit*. Fast cars, beautiful clothes. You're living the dream, man." He sighs before digging into his salad course enthusiastically.

Andre just laughs. "Thank you. This is our goal, to be as the kids say, *fire*. Why is all of the American slang centered around temperature, I wonder? It used to be that things were *cool*, now they're *hot, fire, bomb* or *lit*. Fascinating. I have an entire team of people who study the social media trends."

James looks like he has no idea what is happening. But I strongly suspect that Wallace in his own unique, bumbling way has just broken the ice for us.

Well, if he's broken the ice, I might as well jump in first.

"Mirage employs a lot of talented young designers. It's why our ad campaigns are so on trend. We combine years of experience in understanding what makes people buy with the fresh perspective of different generations."

Mya grins over at me. "Wallace is on Milo's team. He's

been with us for almost a year now and graduated from Columbia with honors. He's also an amateur photographer and is pretty popular on Instagram, too."

I glance over at her. *He is?* How does she know all that?

Maybe there is something to paying attention in those bullshit icebreaker sessions at work after all.

Wallace looks shocked, too. "My account has nowhere near the numbers some of my friends have, but I just passed ten thousand."

Mr. Lavin actually looks impressed. "That's quite an accomplishment, especially for a hobbyist." He clears his throat. "I'm happy to meet with you all in person after hearing about you from Mr. Lawson."

James gives him a tight smile. "I'm extremely proud of my team."

"It shows," Andre replies.

Dinner proceeds with the typical pleasantries. Wallace looks a little confused, but I can only pray the kid can hold his tongue.

With these types of clients, you never rush right into business. You need to woo them, almost like a woman you're trying to convince to come back to your place after dinner. She's not just going to come with you if you ask within the first ten minutes. She needs you to show her that you're worth her time.

Are you going to savor her the same way you do the ten-inch porterhouse on your plate?

Or will you rush through the act like a kid scarfing down an ice cream cone?

I can't imagine a man like Andre Lavin scarfing anything. He needs to see that we're not only the best team to take over his marketing but also that we're people he can work with.

We need him to *like* us.

As the waitress is clearing the entrees, Andre looks around the table with satisfaction. "Perhaps it is old-fashioned, but I care to meet with any agencies that work on our marketing directly. It's important that the people crafting our image understand what we're about here at Lavin Couture."

Everyone instantly ceases their side conversations and pays attention. Now we're getting to the good stuff. The reason we're all here.

"What is your vision for the company, Mr. Lavin?" Mya asks. "I've read the official mission statement, but I would love to hear it from you."

"Please, call me Andre."

The way he's looking at her makes it clear he just wants to hear her say his name.

My hand sitting on top of the table curls into a fist. It shouldn't bother me. He's just a client, throwing a little charm at the pretty ad executive. I've seen it plenty of times, and I've had my fair share of clients, male and female, attempt to flirt with me.

None of those made me want to growl in frustration. Or made me worry that Mya might actually want to flirt back.

"It's much more than just the clothes," Andre begins after a brief pause. "Our brand creates the garments that become part of people's memories. And for our newest venture, we're looking for a partner that understands the importance of family, friendship, love."

The woman sitting next to him sniffs. *Cristiane Laveque.* From my research on the Lavin team, I know that she's a top designer for Lavin Couture.

"Apologies, but this is not a strength of American companies, we have found. So few understand *l'amore.*" She shakes her head ruefully as if the vulgar ways of the American market are just too much.

Mentally, I'm rolling my eyes, but this could be a real obstacle to winning their business. If they think that we're not cultured enough, it will be difficult to change that opinion. Granted, Mirage does plenty of "American" commercials and brands, but it's not like we're all race cars and beer. We have plenty of upper-echelon brands in the jewelry, hotel and entertainment industries.

"I believe Mirage can handle anything. We have such a diverse workforce that all of our clients find someone they can relate to. We also have more women in leadership roles than many of our competitors."

Maybe that'll calm her fears that we don't get *l'amore*. Mya in particular handles a lot of brands that cater to women, including a high-profile lingerie line.

Andre sits back in his chair and seems to be considering her words. "I must admit we've been approached by other firms that are run by people who are married. They understand what brides want."

James sits up straighter. "So, it is a bridal line?"

Andre laughs lightly. "Yes, the rumors are true. Lavin Couture will introduce a new line called Lavin Bridal next year. It will be a separate division of the company which is why I'm meeting with investors. I didn't want word to get out until it was all finalized."

James looks like he's going to be sick. This is why Elizabeth has been so smug. She must have heard the Lavin group wanted someone who has been through the process of planning a wedding. Just another way for her to rub her recent marriage in James's face.

"I'm sure all the women on our team have mentally planned their dream wedding, even if they aren't married." I send a panicked glance at Mya.

This would be a really good fucking time for her to pipe in with some story of how she's been dreaming of her wedding dress since she was a little girl.

Unfortunately, Andre seems to be following my line of thought because he turns directly to Mya, too. "If you were planning a wedding, for example," he says, "wouldn't you want a wedding planner who was married?"

Mya pauses with her water glass halfway to her mouth. "Well, yes. I suppose I would."

James just blinks. Wallace pauses mid-chew with a piece of iceberg lettuce hanging from his lip. The whole table seems stunned into silence. She didn't mean to say that, and everyone can see it on her face. But in a rare, caught-off-guard moment, Mya has done the unforgivable.

She's been honest.

An awkward silence descends over the table. James takes another gulp from his scotch. Across from me, members of the Lavin team exchange significant glances before taking an interest in their plates.

Worst of all, Andre Lavin just looks amused.

Meanwhile, Mya looks devastated.

You know how sometimes you can look back and identify the precise moment you fucked up? Well, later tonight I'm sure I'll be remembering the exact second I pushed us all off the cliff together.

"I agree," I state loudly.

James chokes slightly, and Wallace pounds him on the back. I ignore his panicked look and keep my eyes on Mr. Lavin.

"I agree with Mya," I repeat in case anyone at the table missed it the first time I pushed my career in front of a bus. "Having a married wedding planner would be great. Although I'd be more concerned about the people actually doing the work. That's really what sets Mirage apart."

By now, everyone is staring at me, especially James, probably wondering where the hell I'm going with this.

Mya, however, is watching me with a small, tremulous smile on her face. Like she can't believe that I'm backing her up right now. And damn if that smile isn't what does me in.

Because I don't just bet on distracting Mr. Lavin, I double down and take it all the way to the bank.

"Mirage is really the best fit for anything to do with weddings. After all, it's the only agency I know with two team leads that are in love and engaged to be married." I turn to Mya and whisper, "Just go with it."

Then I tilt my head slightly and brush my lips over hers.

seven

MYA

EVERYONE IS STARING. I can feel the heat of their eyes on the side of my face. But even that isn't enough to take me out of this moment. This sweet, thrilling moment. My eyes drift closed, and the world falls away.

Milo is kissing me.

If you'd asked me just an hour ago what kind of kisser I thought Milo would be, I'd have said aggressive. He's all about going all-in and getting to the finish line. I would have assumed that he wouldn't care much about the process but rather only about the end game.

I would have been completely and utterly wrong.

His lips are soft, and he feathers them over mine gently, barely touching me. The result is a whispery soft touch that sends chills up and down my spine. Then he lays his mouth over mine and kisses me properly, his tongue brushing softly against mine.

After what feels like several hours but is probably only several seconds, he pulls back. But he doesn't just stop. No, Milo can't do anything simply, not even shocking me to my core with a kiss. Because right after he pulls away, he does this soft little nuzzle, rubbing his nose back and forth against mine.

Why is that my kryptonite?

That completely unnecessary little snuggle just takes all the indignation I was building up to and scatters it into the wind. Along with all rational thought.

A throat clears and it's like jumping into an ice bath. If we'd been standing, we'd have probably sprung apart, but instead I grope the table blindly until my hand connects with my water glass. The icy liquid cools my throat but not my lust.

What the hell was that?

Everyone at the table is still eating and talking softly amongst themselves, almost like the last thirty seconds didn't just change the rotational orbit of the planet. Isn't it funny how a certain event can knock you off your feet but seems to have no effect on anyone else? It's like experiencing an earthquake while everyone around you goes on with their lives unaware.

Well, everyone isn't unaware. Andre Lavin is watching us carefully.

So is James.

Oh shit.

This is where I should speak up. Tell Mr. Lavin that I cannot wait to see his newest designs, that women everywhere are going to be clamoring for the chance to wear one of his dresses. But I can't because my mind is still muddled, and I can still feel the imprint of Milo's lips against mine.

"You make an interesting point, Mr. Hamilton. Being married is one thing, but to have a couple who are currently planning a wedding designing my campaign would be ideal."

Mr. Lavin nods in satisfaction.

"I had a good feeling about this firm, but I can see that your reputation is accurate. Professional, innovative and discreet. Exactly what I need."

James looks slightly dazed, the same expression you might wear after you narrowly miss being hit by a cab. He looks between me and Milo and then back to Mr. Lavin, but nothing comes out of his mouth.

Once again, Wallace comes to the rescue. "You can't go wrong with those two in charge, if you're looking for discretion. They've been dating in secret for ages and nobody knew except for me. I mean, I could tell. He stares at her ass whenever she walks away."

The water I just sipped comes back up my nose.

Milo hands me a napkin without missing a beat. "Thank you, Wallace. So, Mr. Lavin, tell us about your vision for Lavin Bridal in particular."

And so it goes.

Milo manages to carry the conversation all the way through the dessert course and then through coffee. Personally, I've never understood the practice of drinking coffee after dessert, but when the waitress comes around, I order some anyway.

Maybe the extra caffeine will wake me the hell up.

But I still feel like I'm sleepwalking as James bids the members of the Lavin team goodnight and they promise to be in touch. Wallace is the first to scamper off, probably to go post the selfie he took with Mr. Lavin to Instagram. The thought makes me chuckle, but my throat instantly turns to sandpaper when James approaches.

This entire time, Milo and I have been sitting in silence. I couldn't take the chance of asking any questions where the Lavin team might overhear. But now I wish I'd thought to text him or something so I'd know how we're handling this.

But James doesn't look upset at all. He's practically glowing. It could be all the scotch, but either way, he looks thrilled.

"You two, ah, I should have known. You've done an amazing job keeping your relationship out of the office. Good work. Knew I could count on you." He claps Milo on the shoulder and gifts me with a wide, loopy grin.

Even if I knew what to say to him right now, I don't think I'd have the heart to wipe that smile off his face. Tomorrow is soon enough for him to realize that we've screwed up this deal.

Maybe a good night's sleep will make him more lenient when he's deciding whether to fire us.

Milo pulls out my chair for me as I stand, and I follow wordlessly as we leave the restaurant. It's a Thursday night, but as we walk back through the casino to reach the elevators to the rooms, there are so many people out you'd never think it was a weekday. Time seems to move differently here.

There's an older lady with a purple fanny pack methodically feeding coins into a slot machine. She looks like she's been at it for a while.

Maybe I should just stay down here, living off the free drinks and the adrenaline of gambling. It would probably be better than what's waiting for me when we get back to DC.

I'm so deep in my thoughts that I'm not paying attention when we get on the elevator. It's only when it stops that I realize we didn't push the button for my floor. But Milo loops his arm around my waist and guides me out of the elevator anyway.

"But my room—"

"Not here," he murmurs in my ear. The deep rumble of his voice so close sends a shiver down my spine. "Some of the Lavin team are on this floor. Wait until we get inside."

"Inside what?"

Belatedly, I realize he means inside his room. He has his key card out and the door open before I can say, *No way in hell*.

The door slams shut behind us, and all the things I was getting ready to say get stuck in my throat.

Trying to gather my thoughts, I look around the room. The layout is the same as the one I was given, TV, big window directly across from the door, except he has a king-size bed instead of two doubles. Behind him, there are several dress shirts scattered on the bed, and the covers are all tangled, like he took a nap before coming down to dinner.

Just like that I have a mental image of Milo naked in those sheets, and being alone with him in this room seems like a *very* bad idea.

Completely at ease with the idea of the two of us being alone, he shrugs out of his suit jacket and loosens his tie. I'm instantly distracted by the small patch of skin revealed at the top of his shirt where it's unbuttoned. "I know you must have a million questions," he says finally.

But I don't. Truthfully, I only have one.

"What the hell just happened?"

eight

MILO

"WHAT JUST HAPPENED IS I secured a multimillion-dollar ad account for our agency. I just saved both our jobs."

She snorts delicately. "You just lied to a potential client and to our boss! Besides, since when have you ever cared about *my* career?"

There it is again, the veiled accusation that I've hurt her somehow. I move closer, noticing how her eyes focus on my lips.

"Why would you think I don't care about your career? Tell me, I can see you're dying to since you keep bringing it up. What did I do that was so bad?"

That seems to take the cork out of whatever was holding her back. Arms flying, she gets all up in my face, and damn if it isn't the sexiest thing watching her march around while that clingy dress drapes around her.

"You stole the Adler account after I told you how much I wanted it! Six months. That's how long I spent researching them and planning for how we would approach them. And then James asked *you* to approach the client."

By the time she's finished, my mouth is hanging open and I'm experiencing something that I don't feel often. Remorse.

"Mya, I'm going to tell you something. You probably won't believe it, but I need you to understand that I'm being completely genuine." I pause. "I'm a clueless jerk sometimes."

She crosses her arms. "I won't have trouble believing that."

"But you might have trouble believing that I didn't realize you wanted the Adler account for yourself."

Her eyes fire up again, but I hold up a hand before she can respond. "Just let me explain. When you first told me about the Adler account, I was already handling two other jewelers, remember?"

She nods reluctantly.

"We used to do that all the time, right? I'd see an account that I thought would be perfect for you, so I'd mention it. You'd do the same for me. We were friends once. Or at least, I thought we were."

The anger on her face has softened somewhat. "We were friends. That's why it hurt so much. I thought you knew how much I wanted that account."

"I truly didn't, but that's on me. Because that means I wasn't listening well enough, and I'm sorry."

Then, because I know it will make her laugh, I add, "But if it makes you feel any better, Owen Adler has a serious flatulence problem. So you can take over those update meetings if you really want to."

Mya covers her eyes with her hands. "No, thank you. I got a little preview of that the last time he was in the office. Maybe the universe was doing me a favor in that particular case."

"Probably. So many things make sense now. I had no idea you wanted that account. No wonder you hate me."

Mya blushes. "I don't hate you. Not really."

The tension in the room goes down several notches, but I can sense that I'm still on thin ice with her. Not surprising since she's spent the last two years thinking I fucked her over on purpose.

And she just saw me lie to our boss, a potential client, and several of our colleagues.

"Look, this thing with the Lavin team is a win-win situation. He likes us, and that's half the battle. Now that we're in, he'll schedule another meeting for us to present how we'd handle marketing for the new line."

"This is never going to work! Everyone knows we're not actually together."

It's amazing to me that she has this much faith in people after working in advertising for so long.

"Mya, have you forgotten what we do for a living? We make people see what we want them to see. People will believe whatever we tell them if we put on a show. Reality is what we say it is. If we say we're together, then we're together."

"And when people ask where my engagement ring is?"

"If anyone asks, we'll tell them we haven't found the perfect ring yet. Done. Handled."

She shakes her head and sits on the edge of the bed. "It's that simple for you, huh?"

I reach down and adjust the bulge in my pants which has been stuck at an uncomfortable angle ever since I kissed her downstairs.

"Believe me, nothing about this is simple. This is going to be the hardest thing I've ever done," I add, putting extra emphasis on the *hard*.

She laughs, but her cheeks darken slightly again. Damn, messing with her is fun. It's so easy to get her flustered. Mya is such an interesting personality, equal parts ballbuster and blushing schoolgirl.

"Don't think you're distracting me from the most important thing here. Who gets lead on the account?"

I grin, having known she wasn't going to forget that. That's my girl, all flash and fire and tough as nails. She might blush when I tease her, but she's not going to let anything slip by her.

Mya loves to win just as much as I do, something that I never would have thought would turn me on in a woman. But competing with her is almost as sexy as the thought of…

She narrows her eyes at me as if she can hear my thoughts.

"We'll each come up with a full campaign to present to the Lavin team. That's usually what we do anyway, right? Well in this case, no one will know except for us who created each campaign. Mr. Lavin will choose whichever one he likes better, and that's who will lead the account."

She appears to be thinking about it. "We let the work speak for itself. James is happy. The client is happy. I like it."

"It's the best way. Lavin Couture deserves the best that Mirage has to offer, and obviously that's going to come from either me or you." I sit on the bed next to her, noticing how she goes still.

"You really believe that?"

I nod. "Yes. We may not always agree on our methods, but your work is exceptional, Mya. What you did for Fallen Angel Cosmetics was brilliant."

She smiles. "I liked your campaign for Murray's Tires, too. Who would have thought tires could be sexy?"

I laugh at that. "This is what I miss the most from when we were friends. When you love what you do, that's a reward in and of itself. But there's nothing like being able to share it with someone else. To explain the methodology behind why you made a certain design choice or went in a certain direction, and then know that they understand, it's thrilling."

Mya looks shocked, and I'm suddenly self-conscious about being so open. But it's true, everything I said. That kind of synergy is definitely not something I'll find with the Brittanys or the Jessicas of the world.

That's something I've only ever had with Mya, actually.

"I like talking to you, too. Well, not when you're trying to drive me up the wall. But those other times, before everything went off the rails... It meant a lot to me, too."

Mya's eyes soften, like she's remembering, and I like that look on her.

While we've been talking, we've subconsciously moved closer to each other, and when she peeks up at me, she's so close I can feel her soft breath on my chin. All at once, she seems to realize how close we are and stands suddenly.

"I should go!"

"Not yet. Some of the Lavin team are staying on this

floor, remember? We want them to believe we're really in *l'amore*."

Mya throws up her hands. "Well, how are we supposed to convince them of that?"

"For starters, they would expect us to share a room. They would expect us to want to share a room." I wiggle my eyebrows at her. "Maybe we should rock the bed and scream a lot."

I'm expecting her to laugh with me, maybe make a joke about screaming my name. But instead, she just looks skeptical.

Uncomfortable.

She shakes her head. "Like that's believable. That only happens in the movies."

"Are you saying you've never screamed during sex before?"

Now, I don't want to overstate my case here, but I don't think it's a secret that I know my way around a woman's body. There are few things more satisfying than watching a woman lose her inhibitions, melt against you, and yes, scream your name.

So when I see that look on Mya's face, the truth of the situation hits me with all the subtlety of a two-by-four.

Prim, perfect Mya Taylor has never had that kind of sex in real life.

And every part of me is dying to know how that is possible.

Fuck me.

MYA

CONSIDERING how many things have gone wrong tonight, you'd think it couldn't get much worse, but apparently we haven't reached our quota on weirdness for the night. Standing in a hotel room alone with Milo while he talks about screaming during sex takes it to a whole different level.

Especially since the way he's watching me makes it clear he's not going to just let this go.

"Have you?" he presses again, his eyes locked on mine.

This is *not* happening. I'm not talking about orgasms while he stares at me like that. Just not doing it.

"I'm hardly a virgin, Milo."

His face twists into a grimace. "Jesus, don't say that."

"What? I just said–"

"What you said was a bullshit attempt to deflect and not

answer. Which tells me everything I need to know." He runs his hands through his hair, looking pissed off, which makes no sense to me.

"How did we go from discussing your bad behavior at dinner to talking about my love life?" *My non-existent love life*, I think ruefully.

A guy like Milo probably goes through women like underwear. What would he say if he knew it's been six months since I've been laid?

Or kissed.

Or hugged.

Or touched.

Great, now he's got me thinking about how pathetic I am.

"I'm just trying to understand what the fuck is happening in the world that a woman like you is having bad sex. Any man lucky enough to see you naked should be putting in the work to take you to O-town every time."

Something in my expression must tip him off because suddenly he stops pacing and stares at me. "Mya, you've *had* an orgasm before, haven't you?"

Now we've crossed the line from inappropriate to just straight-up embarrassing.

"Of course, I have. Not that it's any of your business."

He still looks disturbed, but at least he's no longer

looking at me like some kind of space alien, which is why I have no idea what possesses me to say what I do next.

"Just not while anyone else is there," I mumble softly.

"Fuck me!" he explodes before whirling around to blink at me in disbelief. His mouth opens and closes several times before he makes a strangled growling sound that has me going instantly wet. "Fucking hell."

"Fucking isn't the problem," I snap, mortification at what I've admitted starting to sink in.

Of all the people I could have confided in, why would I tell Milo?

For years it's been my secret shame and the real reason my ex didn't want to "settle" with me. I've read every Cosmo article, tried yoga and hypnosis and even those weird-ass positions in the illustrated Kama Sutra I ordered online. William was offended when I suggested using a vibrator in bed, and he didn't even seem to like when I touched myself.

Maybe that was the problem. It all felt like work instead of fun. And right now, it just feels like one more way I don't measure up.

Especially with the way Milo is looking at me.

"You know what? I'm done talking about this. It's been a long night, and we're probably both going to be out of a job tomorrow once James sobers up and comes to his senses. So for now, I'm going to my room to get comfortable."

He springs forward and grabs my arm. "Wait, Mya. I'm serious about not leaving yet. I'm pretty sure Christiane is staying on this floor. She seems predisposed to hate us already."

Fed up with being told what to do, I reach behind me and unzip my dress. "I need to get out of this bra before it cuts off my circulation." I raise my eyebrows, waiting to see what he'll do.

But he shocks the hell out of me when he calls my bluff. Milo grabs one of the discarded dress shirts from the bed and hands it to me. "Change into this. You can order room service and relax just as easily here as you can in your room."

Clearly, like most men, Milo has no idea what relaxation means for a woman. But I'm just embarrassed and exhausted enough not to care anymore.

So I take the shirt and escape into the safe haven of the bathroom. Once the door is closed and locked behind me, I meet my own eyes in the mirror. That was the most ridiculous conversation, but strangely cathartic, too.

Maybe I just needed to tell someone, and Milo happened to be the unlucky bystander when it all came bursting forth.

Not that he should have acted like it was such a bother to him. I'm the one who's been sexually frustrated for years, after all.

If anyone has cause to be annoyed by the situation, it's *me*.

The bathrooms in this hotel come stocked with all manner of toiletries, so I use the mini facial bar to wash my makeup off. There's a small hook on the back of the door, so I use that to hang my dress by the straps and put on the shirt Milo gave me. It's a good thing he's so tall or there would be no way this thing would fit over my chest, but it's just big enough. Although I have to unbutton quite a bit at the top so I don't feel like my boobs are being strangled.

After pulling the pins out of my bun, I finger comb my hair down around my face. It's super thick, so it's easier to keep it braided or in a bun, but when I'm relaxing, I just let it go wild. Milo will just have to deal.

He's the one who wouldn't let me leave, so if he doesn't like it, he can bite me.

The man looked like he wanted to bite you anyway.

With that thought, I yank open the bathroom door and march back out into the room. Milo looks up from the mini bar where he's selected a small bottle. His mouth falls open slightly before he clears his throat and looks away, guiltily.

"Want a drink?"

"Uh, sure."

"We have scotch, some dubious-looking wine, and vodka."

I shrug. "Alcohol. Anything that can make me forget the past three hours."

He's about to respond when my phone rings. To my surprise, Milo picks it up as if he has every right to know who's calling me. He tilts the screen so I can see the face. A picture of me and William taken during our last New Year's Eve flashes on the screen. I take the phone and hit the button to silence the call.

"I never got around to changing the picture on his profile," I blurt.

Then I'm instantly mad at myself for explaining. I don't have to justify why I have a picture of my ex on my phone.

"He's called twice already. Some men really don't know the meaning of no, do they?"

I climb back on the bed, satisfied when Milo's eyes follow the movement of my legs. He hasn't invited me to take over his bed, but oh well. This is what you get when you stand between a girl and her chill time. I settle back against the pillows and snuggle into the cozy sheets.

"William wasn't too good at listening in general," I admit.

"Enough about him. What did you think of the rest of the Lavin team? Obviously, Christiane hates us. But otherwise?"

To my surprise, we spend the next hour talking about everything related to Lavin Couture. It's not a surprise to me that Milo has researched their prior campaigns, but he also looked up human interest stories about the brand and found out what their charitable initiatives are. That's one that I hadn't thought of yet. Then I tell him about the collaborations Mr. Lavin did before he started the brand. That was something Milo hadn't thought of.

In the midst of it all, I can't help thinking that we make a pretty damn good team.

"Can I ask you something?" Milo asks when there's a lull in the conversation. We've been sitting quietly for a few minutes, but it's a good kind of silence. The comfortable kind where you don't feel any pressure to perform and you can just *be*.

"Sure. I mean you've already asked the embarrassing stuff, like how I like my orgasms. How much further down the rabbit hole can we go?"

His smile awakens something in me that I didn't know was dormant, and I press my thighs together to stop the ache. But as usual, Milo is tuned in to everything I'm feeling. His eyes drop to the juncture between my thighs, and his blue eyes darken. When he speaks, his voice is one shade above a growl.

"Why did you stay with a guy who didn't satisfy you? One who made you feel that you had to wear long skirts and hide yourself? I'm trying to understand, but I just don't get it. You're so strong. I can't imagine you taking shit from anybody."

This is the kind of conversation we probably shouldn't be having when I'm dressed in only his shirt and snuggled next to him on a bed. Maybe it's the mini-bar wine stealing away the last fucks I had to give, but I just don't care anymore.

"Even strong women get lonely," I say finally. "Will isn't a bad guy, just an oblivious one. He wanted something I couldn't give him. Do you know what he said to me at the end?"

He turns over so he's now facing me directly. "What?"

"He said that settling down with me felt too much like settling. Like I was the consolation prize he'd accepted when he couldn't find anything better."

If you'd asked me before that moment, I'd have told you I was over it and that Will's words didn't have any power over me. But saying it to Milo in that moment was different, like I could actually admit how much it had hurt.

"Now he's trying to get you back. You know why?"

I shake my head through the tears that have suddenly sprung to my eyes.

He tips up my chin. "Because he's finally wised up and discovered how lucky he was to even have a chance with you. A chance that he won't get again. You are one of a kind, Mya Taylor. You are no one's fucking consolation prize."

My phone rings again, and the picture of Will and me flashes on the screen. Milo looks down at the phone and then up at me.

"May I?"

I have no idea what he means, so I shrug. He grabs the phone and swipes right to answer.

"Yes. No, you have the right number, this is Mya's phone. This is her fiancé."

My mouth falls open.

"That's right, her *fiancé*. A guy who is smart enough to know exactly how special she is and how lucky I am to be with her. A chance you won't have again, so please fuck all the way off and stop calling."

He pulls the phone away, but then before he disconnects, he puts it back to his ear. "And by the way, pal, her kneecaps are *fantastic*."

Then he drops the phone back on the bed and his mouth crashes down on mine.

MILO

IT'S GO TIME.

I settle gently on top of Mya, not wanting to shock her out of the moment. Maybe it hasn't fully sunk in for her yet that she's kissing me, the dude she's hated for years and the guy who just put her in the middle of a big fat lie. Either way, I don't want to waste the opportunity I've been dreaming of since the day we met. I want to show Mya how good we could be together.

Her nails dig into my arms, and I love that she's just as into this as I am. The phone is ringing non-stop now, and the thought of her jackass ex calling while I'm currently worshipping her mouth makes me smile.

Mya opens her eyes when she feels my lips move against hers. "Why are you smiling?"

"Because I'm kissing you. It doesn't take more than that, beautiful."

I kiss her again, just because I can. Because we're here and for once she's smiling at me instead of insulting me, and I'm afraid if I blink things will go back to the way they were. Mya's hands dive into my hair, and my eyes almost roll into the back of my head.

If just her touch on my hair feels this good, I'll probably blow my load before she even gets below the belt.

Then she stops.

"Wait. This is not a good idea."

I push my hips forward, reminding her of where I am. In this position, she can feel all of me resting right against her stomach.

Hey, what do you want me to say? A guy has to use every advantage he has.

"Feels like a good idea to me."

The movement of our bodies has pushed the fabric of the shirt up, and I can see her panties. A little pink scrap that might as well be a red flag in front of a bull. Her head falls back, and she lets out the sexiest little moan as I grind against her. But then her hand goes to the middle of my chest.

"I don't want this to get in the way of work. Sleeping with a coworker is always a bad idea. Plus, there's no point. It's not like a relationship between us could go anywhere."

My mood drops slightly. The thought of relationships usually cause that effect. But then again, I'm not really turned off by the thought of a relationship with Mya at all.

Which is a shock. I'm more annoyed that she doesn't think a relationship between us would work out.

Strange, I know.

No time to examine that now. There's something more important to discuss.

"I promise you that this chemistry between us absolutely has a point, and it has nothing to do with the future. People have sex even if it's not going anywhere."

"Maybe other people do. I don't. What's the point?" Mya really looks bewildered.

If she'd said that earlier, I would have been caught off guard. But now that I know her past situation with her ex-dickhead, I get it. She's not used to the idea of sex being a pleasurable thing.

Which is something I can definitely fix.

"Because with the right man, it's mind-blowing. I can prove it to you." I lean down and kiss her neck.

"I seriously doubt that." But her voice trembles slightly when my tongue darts out to touch the pulse thumping right below her skin.

"Let's make a little wager then because my mouth doesn't write checks my body can't cash. We're going to be working closely together to lock down this account. I propose that we use that time to work on a little side project, as well."

"Side project?" She looks skeptical.

"Yeah. Operation *Teach Mya about Multiple Orgasms.*"

Her husky laugh forces the rest of the blood in my body to flow south. Goddamn, what I want to do to this woman. I'm thinking dirty thoughts, and she's laughing at me.

"I bet I could give it to you so good, you'd beg me for more."

Her eyes flash with heat. "*You wish.* I'll never beg."

This woman. Clearly, she doesn't know that there are few things I love more than a challenge. And the opportunity to have her calling out for more, begging me to take her, is too good to resist.

"Are you willing to find out?" I raise my eyebrows.

She glares at me and then looks away. "Fine. Not like it matters. I think I know my own body better than you do."

"I guess we'll see about that, won't we?"

Mya's breath stops when my fingers go to the buttons on the front of the shirt. The top two are already open so I pop the next one out. I watch her face, waiting to see if she's okay with this, but when our eyes meet, she nods slowly. My heart crashes inside my chest at the green light.

She's into this.

"Milo–" Her next words are swallowed when our lips meet again.

Why did we wait so long to do this?

Years of bickering back and forth when we could have been working that tension off after work together. Even today, she thought she was calling my bluff when she changed out of her dress and into my shirt, but that's because she had no idea what the sight of her in white cotton would do to me.

Mya in a plain dress shirt is sexier than any other woman wearing skimpy lingerie.

Which brings me back to what she is or *isn't* wearing beneath my shirt right now.

With every button that I pull free, another inch of golden-brown skin is revealed. This close, I'm surrounded by her fragrance, and I want nothing more than to lick her up, taste the unique scent of Mya direct from the source. But I don't want to scare her off by moving too fast, so I content myself with just looking at first.

Then the sides of the shirt fall open completely, and her full breasts pop into view.

Going slow is no longer an option.

"Milo! Oh my god."

She moans when I take her breast into my mouth and suck hard. Her breasts are perfect, full and round, just like I knew they'd be. I can't wait any longer to find out if the rest of her is just as perfect. My hand inches over the soft skin of her thigh until I reach her panties. The material is so wet and hot I can feel the heat before I even get there.

"Fuck, you're soaked for me already."

Mya's fingers clench in my hair. "I can't help it," she moans.

"Oh, I don't want you to help it, baby. That's exactly how I want you, wet and ready for me. And you'll take it all, won't you?"

She nods frantically, and I can see that she's already halfway gone. My fingers have been stroking her through the cotton panel of her panties this whole time, rubbing it against her, using the fabric to increase the friction. But as good as this feels, I have to know that she's really okay with this.

The thought of her regretting this later hits me right in the chest.

I can't bear the thought of her remembering this as a mistake. What could happen between us should never be thought of as anything other than heaven.

"Mya, baby, look at me."

Her eyelashes flutter as she struggles to open her eyes. I'm hit with a feeling of warmth as her brown eyes lock on mine, and her gaze is filled with desire, confusion, and something that looks like trust.

"I need to know, is this what you want?"

God help me if she changes her mind, but I'll take the

worst case of blue balls in history over doing anything that would hurt Mya.

She hesitates briefly, but then a look of determination comes over her face. "What you described before... It's never been like that for me. I do want this. I want you."

"Then you'll have me. You'll have it all."

———

I'M sure she thought I'd jump right into it. But what she doesn't understand is that I've just been given the keys to the ultimate playground. Mya is a buffet of tempting curves and sweet swells. I'm not going to waste a moment of this.

Before we're through, I'll have mapped every inch of her skin, tasted every soft crevice and coaxed out every drop of her pleasure.

Then I'll do it all over again.

First, I help her out of my shirt. I have the perfect angle to admire her, the sinuous curves of her waist leading into her hips, the smooth column of her throat as she arches her back, the rich dark spill of her hair, a stunning contrast to the caramel tone of her skin. I'm almost overwhelmed, not sure where to start when I want to devour her whole.

"Open your legs for me. Yes, that's it. Open those pretty thighs."

She blushes but allows her legs to fall open. Now that

the shirt's no longer in the way, I can see the damp spot on her panties clearly. My head falls forward as I take a minute to compose myself.

Something about this woman ramps me up faster than anything.

If I'm not careful, I'll go too fast and cheat her out of the experience she deserves. That's the last thing I want to do.

She flushes as I watch her, and I can see the effort it takes for her not to close her legs and hide. But we're not doing this under the covers in the dark.

Hell no.

I want her to see everything.

Feel everything.

"You are so beautiful." I move closer and inhale as I lower myself between her thighs.

Her legs start to close, but the breadth of my shoulders keeps them open. I can feel that she's starting to tense up again, so I press a gentle kiss to the soft skin of her stomach. She sighs softly and relaxes back into the pillows.

"And so wet." My hand finds its way back to where it was before, but this time I'm not content just to stroke her through the fabric. I tug the cloth to the side and almost come just from how hot and wet she is against my fingers.

"It's a fucking crime that you've been hiding this from me."

I push two fingers inside, and her muscles clamp down

on the intrusion so tight that my dick twitches in jealousy. It wants to be where my lucky fingers are right now, being massaged and squeezed by the tightest little pussy I've ever felt.

"I haven't been hiding," Mya gasps when I rotate my hand, my fingers probing–

"Oh my god!" she whispers when I find the soft spot I'm searching for. Her eyes drift shut, and she shivers uncontrollably as I massage her G-spot. While her eyes are closed, I lean down and cover her with my mouth.

Desire slams through me. Salty and sweet, her taste is like warm apple pie on a cold day. I'm almost feral now as my lips latch on to her clit, my fingers working counterpoint to the rhythmic lashing of my tongue. Mya tenses, and then her pussy muscles go wild, squeezing my fingers.

Her response has the effect of throwing gasoline on a fire that's already out of control.

She's still whimpering from the aftereffects of her orgasm when I stand and push my pants down. Mya gets up on her knees, and her hands move over my chest frantically, trying to unbutton my shirt as fast as she can. Buttons go flying as she rips through the last few, and finally, I'm naked.

She sucks in a breath. "Damn."

I laugh at her loss for words. "Trust me, you're saying what I've been thinking this whole time."

Then neither of us is laughing anymore as I climb back

on the bed with her. "I don't think we need these anymore." I tug at the edge of her panties. Mya lifts her hips and pushes them down, kicking them away.

It hits me then, the gravity of what we're about to do.

I mean, this is Mya. The woman I've been dreaming about for the last two years, and my reluctant crush, for lack of a better term. Even when I was fooling myself that we hated each other, my dick was never on that program. He's always loved her.

Now I'm going to be the first man who gets to make her come.

You cannot fuck this up.

I caress her from her waist down to her thigh, my fingers trailing gently over her skin. "I love how you feel."

"I love how I feel, too. I've never been so satisfied." She smiles lazily, stretching under my fingers like a cat.

I wouldn't be surprised to hear her purring. It's a heady feeling, watching her all flushed and content from her orgasm. I could get used to seeing her like this.

She stretches again, drawing my attention back to her breasts. Her nipples are dusky, standing out against her skin like chocolate candies on caramel. I get up quickly and find the package of condoms in my luggage. Mya watches with unabashed curiosity as I smooth the latex on.

I lean over the bed and kiss the fragrant skin above her heart. It beats against my lips, increasing in tempo as I nuzzle the underside of her breast. It increases to a gallop as I move between her thighs. We both tremble at the contact.

I don't move as my mouth explores the skin behind her ear, the curve of her throat. I take my time with tiny nips to her jawline before my tongue slips between her lips. My mouth covers hers again, licking and biting. She whimpers as I suck her tongue.

"What are you doing? Make love to me." She squirms beneath me, and it takes all my willpower to remain still.

I need her as crazy as she makes me.

I need her to *need* me.

To crave what only my body can give her.

"Milo?" She hits me in the shoulder, but I continue tormenting the skin on her neck.

I haven't heard it yet. The words I'm waiting for.

She lets out a soft groan as I circle my hips, my cock rocking against her clit over and over again. I can tell by the uneven hitch in her breathing that she's close.

Very close.

Then she finally says the words I've been waiting to hear.

"Milo, stop teasing me." Her eyes fix on mine, and she licks her lips. "I want you. *Please.*"

I thrust inside, and she's so wet she takes me all the way. Her eyes roll into the back of her head as she comes instantly, my name on her lips in a broken cry.

"*Christ,*" I mutter, completely turned on by her utter abandon.

Her pussy clutches me like a wet fist, sucking me back in with each thrust, compelling me to never leave. She's like fire, her body so open and hot. The friction is insane, the way we fit together, igniting nerves I didn't know I had.

"I want to make you beg for it. Want to make you scream." I can barely string two sentences together.

My mind is a tangled mass of lust, obsession, desire, and love. I wanted to seduce her, to show her what sex is supposed to be like, but I feel like I'm the one being schooled.

"I'll beg if I have to. Just as long as you don't stop." She grips my hair roughly, holding me hostage for her kiss. She moans into my mouth, her nails digging into my scalp like miniature daggers.

The sharp bite of pain is a welcome reminder of what's at stake.

Good sex isn't good enough for Mya. I need to show her great.

I roll us so that she's on top. Given her history, I thought I'd have to coax her into this position, but she plants her hands on my chest, rotating her hips. I groan, a desperate and needy sound as she lowers herself on top of me, taking me back in slowly. Her eyes are closed, her mouth open on a pant as she works her pussy over me, trying to accept my entire length.

"Touch yourself." I lift her hands and place them on her breasts.

She looks alarmed at first, but quickly gains confidence, playing with her nipples as she rides me. Her dark hair is a wild mass of curls around her face, and her eyes flutter closed when I rock up against her, like the sensation is too much for her to handle.

I've never seen her more beautiful.

"That's it. Goddamn, you're so sexy." I growl as she pinches her nipples, the tight points standing out like stiff little berries. Her body is so ripe. I want to take my time playing with her, watch her respond to my touch.

I reach between us and press my thumb on her clit, adding more pressure with every stroke. My fingers keep up the steady rhythm until she convulses against me, the pulsing grip of her body triggering my own release. It's sooner than I'd like, but as soon as she clamps down on me, I know I'm too far gone.

My orgasm nails me right at the base of my spine, and I surge against her, completely consumed by shattering waves of pleasure. She falls forward, landing on my chest in a heap.

I sweep her curls to the side, only to see tears on her

cheeks. "You're crying. Did I hurt you?" I kiss the moisture away.

"No, you didn't hurt me." She laughs and puts a hand over her heart. "You just overwhelmed me."

"In a good way though, right?" I exhale with relief when she nods.

She laughs again and pulls back so she can see my face. "You were right."

"I'm always right." I laugh when she pinches my nipple. "Ouch. Okay, I'll bite. What was I right about, beautiful?"

Her gaze is soft as she answers. "With the right man, it is mind-blowing." Then she kisses me gently and curls up against my side as if she hasn't just blown my whole world apart with her shy words.

eleven

MYA

MY WHOLE LIFE has been a lie.

As my breathing finally returns to normal, I snuggle against Milo's side. Before Will, I hadn't had a boyfriend in a few years, so I'm not really sure what's considered good after-sex etiquette. He always fell asleep right after sex and hated when I would try to talk then.

So I'm guessing that jumping up and yelling *SCORE* would probably be the wrong thing to do right now. But honestly, that's how I feel.

Years of believing that I was broken. That sex was this big cosmic joke that everyone was playing on me. That orgasms on TV and in movies were grossly exaggerated.

I'd watch those scenes where women were biting, scratching, and of course screaming, and just roll my eyes at the blatant over dramatization. Worse, I was convinced that they were doing active damage to real women, women like me who were dissatisfied with their partners because they couldn't measure up to the Hollywood ideal.

Well, after the things that have just come out of my mouth, I want to write to the Motion Picture Association of America and tell them they didn't do enough. Because I think I just left this plane of existence, used every four-letter word in the English language and probably a few in a language that doesn't exist yet.

And mortifyingly, I'm pretty sure I begged. Multiple times.

"I'm sorry I lost control at the end. I wanted to make you come at least one more time." His voice is soft but still startles me. I thought he'd fallen asleep.

"You wanted... um, wow. Milo, I came three times. I didn't even know I could do that."

Even though I can't see his face in this position, I can feel his satisfaction at my words, and it makes me feel cherished. It's strange how my experience with a guy who admits he's only after sex has been better than with the man who was supposed to be my husband. Probably because Milo actually cares about how it was for me.

Maybe there's something to what Ariana has been saying this whole time. She's always been freer with her sexuality, and I just couldn't understand how that worked. It made me feel like a judgmental bitch, but I was always a little appalled when she'd bring home random guys or sleep with a friend.

The whole friends-with-benefits thing seemed like an oxymoron to me, but she's always maintained that she's happy with her choices because they're *her choices*. She's not sharing herself with anyone who doesn't make her feel respected.

Meanwhile, I felt morally superior because I was only sleeping with my fiancé who made me feel cheap because I couldn't get off with him.

This whole thing has been eye-opening, to say the least.

My fingers have been playing with the skin on Milo's stomach, so I'm startled when his hand clamps down on mine.

"You have to stop that," he growls.

Will I ever get enough of that rough, gravelly voice? It only sounds like that when he's turned on. The idea that I've made him like that is a heady one.

"Doing what?" I bury my face in his shoulder, suddenly shy.

All the things I said and did are coming back to me, and I'm not sure where to look. Did I really yank his hair? Hit his shoulder? I vaguely recall digging my nails into his back, too.

This violent side of me is surprising. The old Mya

thought sex was supposed to be this gentle wave of sensation.

Instead it's like a tsunami.

"Touching me. I'm trying not to jump on you again because I'm sure you must be sore, but your fingers rubbing right above my dick is not helping the case."

A startled laugh escapes my lips but dies when he snatches the sheet away and his fully erect cock comes back into view. Wowza. Just thinking about the fact that I fit that thing inside me—not only that but rode it and begged for more—is making me wet again.

I cross my legs, something Milo immediately notices.

"You want it again, don't you, beautiful? That sweet little pussy is already aching to take me again."

Good lord, this man's dirty mouth.

"Don't make me say it," I whisper.

His eyes dance as he leans over me. I sigh as his lips land on my neck. How did he discover that's my weak spot so fast? It's like he has some sort of cheat sheet that tells him exactly how to make me fall apart.

"Oh, I won't make you say it. Whatever you want, you can have. All you have to do is ask me nicely."

I growl playfully. This man. Of course, he can't resist poking fun at me. He said he would make me beg, and he wasn't wrong. But he's not the only one who can play dirty.

I sit up and toss my hair over my shoulder before

climbing on top of him. Milo's eyes follow as my breasts swing and bob with my movements.

"You want to hear me beg?" I purr, running one hand down my stomach, stopping right before I hit the good stuff.

His eyes don't leave my hand as he nods.

I bring the same hand slowly back up and hook my pinky finger in my mouth. Once I have his attention again, I place my hands on his chest and crawl forward until our lips almost meet.

"Milo?" Gentle kiss. "Do you know what I want?"

Another gentle kiss. His strangled moan is accompanied by a small twitch of his hips. I place a hand on his cheek and look him right in the eyes. His head moves slowly back and forth. Like he's hypnotized.

"I want your long, thick, *hard,*" my hand encircles him, "cock inside me right now. Do you want that, too?" My thumb brushes over the head as he struggles to nod even as he groans at the erotic touch. "You do? Well, maybe *you* should beg *me* for it."

In the span of a heartbeat, he flips us over.

"You're a hell of a quick learner, Miss Taylor. Because when you have my dick in your hand, you can have anything you want."

I'm laughing until he puts me up on my knees and fucks me from behind. But that's okay because I still have a smile on my face even after he makes me scream his name.

twelve

MILO

I RETREAT to the other side of the room, my cell phone clamped to my ear. This is not my normal post-sex behavior, I assure you, but after spending the past thirty minutes just staring at Mya, I'm certifiably freaked out.

Because I don't want to do my usual. I don't want to sneak out before she wakes up. What I want is to watch as she makes those adorable little snuffling noises and then wake her up so we can do it all over again.

"Something had better be on fire," Ethan growls when he finally answers the phone. This is my third time calling.

"Is it technically illegal to force a coworker to marry you?" I bite my lip when Mya lets out a loud sigh and then rolls over to face the other direction. I walk closer to the front door of the room, hoping I won't wake her just yet.

Not until I figure out what alien force has hijacked my brain.

"Okay, I need you to run that by me again. It's the middle of the fucking night, Milo. What the fuck?"

Apparently, he's just realized what time it is.

"You heard me. I need some advice. Legal advice."

He sighs. "I don't think legal advice is what you need. What is going on? You're supposed to be in Vegas right now with James."

"I *am* in Vegas," I hiss as quietly as possible.

"Did you meet some stripper and decide to throw it all away for love? And why are you whispering?"

I glance behind me to where Mya is sleeping peacefully in my bed. "Because I don't want her to hear me."

"Who?"

"Mya."

There's a long pause, and I can hear Ethan shuffling around. Then a few seconds later, I hear him come back. "Okay, I had to get up for this. Something tells me I'm not getting any more sleep tonight. Now, what the hell is going on?"

With permission granted, I launch into the whole long, complicated story starting with James's meltdown in the lobby before dinner and ending with my fake engagement announcement. After I finally pause to take a breath, I hear Ethan chuckling.

"James doesn't pay me enough for this shit," he says finally.

"Thanks for the helpful advice."

"Somehow, I don't think you need me to tell you this is a really bad idea."

"You're my friend. You're supposed to tell me everything is going to be fine. Plus, I figured you'd need a heads-up anyway before we get back and you hear that we're engaged."

"Wait a minute, you mean you're actually going through with it?"

He launches into a rant about sexual harassment and a bunch of other boring shit that I tune out when Mya rolls over again, this time facing me.

Ethan's incredulous voice follows me as I creep closer to the bed to stare at her. Her hair flows all around her face, surrounding her like a dark halo. One hand rests on the pillow next to her cheek. A strange feeling comes over me looking down at her as she sleeps unaware.

So trusting.

I want to be the one who watches over her. Protects her. The idea that after she wakes she might decide to just walk away is torture.

This is a hell of a time to discover that my feelings for Mya Taylor might be about much more than just the physical.

"Uh, what are you doing right now?" Ethan's voice interrupts my thoughts. "Because you're breathing pretty heavily in my ear and it's making me uncomfortable."

I roll my eyes. "I'm watching Mya sleep, and I'm trying not to get caught."

"This is even worse than I thought. Do you hear yourself? You even sound like a creeper."

"Never mind. I don't know why I called you."

"Uh, maybe to keep you out of jail before you do something insane. Well, anything else insane. Sounds like you're already pretty far gone though."

He's right. I'm legitimately off the rails. What the hell is it about Vegas that makes people do crazy things? I lied to, hell, everyone. Then I seduced Mya and had a sexual experience that makes even *me* question whether I've had good sex before.

Now I'm standing in a dark hotel room watching her sleep while thinking about what it would be like to be with Mya for real.

To have the right to wake up next to her and call her mine.

For all this not to be a lie.

"I need to get out of here."

I'm speaking more to myself than to Ethan. Hopefully, he doesn't take it personally when I hang up, suddenly needing to be anywhere but here.

My shoes and dress pants are still in a heap in the middle of the room, so I dress quickly and then turn around looking for a shirt. The one I was wearing is missing buttons from when Mya tore it off me, and I'm for damn sure not putting on the one she was wearing. Having her scent on my skin is definitely not going to help me break free from whatever spell I'm under.

Finally, I grab a clean T-shirt from my bag and throw it on. I look a little odd, I'm sure, wearing dress pants and shoes and a casual shirt, but this is Vegas. You can get away with anything here.

Except, it seems, your heart.

———

I'M SETTLED at the hotel bar with my second drink when I see him.

Andre Lavin walks through the casino with the assurance of someone who is used to getting everything he wants. Warning bells are blaring in the back of my mind. Talking to the client alone would be a red flag on any given day when I've been drinking but especially after everything that went down earlier.

I still haven't forgotten how he looked at Mya. He wants her.

Get in line, buddy.

"Mr. Hamilton. I wasn't expecting to see you again before you left."

Without waiting for an invitation, he takes the seat next to me. The bartender immediately brings him a drink, as if they've just been waiting with his favorite in case he should happen to drop by.

The life of a high roller.

Is this what he's used to, having people fawn all over him all the time? Bringing him whatever he wants?

Whoever he wants?

Anger storms through my system, aided by the amount of alcohol I've had in the past twenty-four hours. I'm not thinking about what's good for my career right now. I'm thinking about what's good for Mya.

"I'm not going to let you treat her like she's some delicacy to be brought on a silver platter," I mumble accusingly.

His lips quirk up at the corners. "Is that right?"

Was I this smug when going after women? God, I hope not, because I really want to punch that grin off his face.

"How long have you worked with your fiancée?"

There's nothing inappropriate about his question, but it feels like a challenge somehow, like he's testing me.

"Two years. She kicks my ass at work, too."

He takes a sip of his drink. "I bet. She seems like a

formidable woman. And quite beautiful. The kind of woman a man has to keep happy."

My fingers clench around my shot glass. "Oh, I keep her happy. In the office and out of it."

His eyes flash as he catches my meaning. His gaze takes in my sloppy dress, and I'm sure he can put two and two together. I look like I've just had sex, quite frankly, with my bedhead and haphazard outfit.

"That's good. Very good. Because there will always be another man waiting if you mess it up."

"I'll handle any marketing questions you have from now on. Stay away from Mya, because I'm not going anywhere."

"Of course, but I felt it only fair to give you notice. It doesn't hurt to let a man know he has some competition."

Now he's just asking to get popped in the mouth.

"Good night, Mr. Hamilton." He leaves a few twenties on the bar and then walks off the way he came.

I'm left with an empty shot glass and no idea what the hell just happened. This whole situation has gotten completely out of hand. I invented this engagement to get the job, and now jealousy might prevent Andre Lavin from hiring us anyway. I wouldn't think he'd allow his personal feelings to play a part in his business decisions, but he's only human.

What if this conversation was his way of warning me that Mirage won't get the job?

James can never know about this. I don't think he would encourage Mya to flirt with a potential client to secure an account, but this is too important to gamble on. I don't want there to be any chance she might be put in that position.

This sex thing between us scrambled my brain a bit, but I have enough wits left to know that work is the most important thing to Mya.

Hell, it's the most important thing to me, too. I might have been feeling sentimental after that intense round upstairs, but that doesn't change who I am or what I want for my future. I put a shaky hand to my chest, trying to calm my suddenly racing heart.

So, it's settled.

I won't say anything to Mya about this either. She doesn't need that pressure. I need to protect her from this.

Not because I feel anything for her beyond desire and friendship.

It's just the right thing to do.

Obviously.

thirteen

MILO

THE TRIP back to DC is much like the trip to Vegas, except Mya and I drop our usual banter and instead treat each other like polite acquaintances. She doesn't make any comments when the flight attendant slips me her number, and I don't make fun of her plastic stress cow.

The whole thing feels fake as hell.

But we've come to an unspoken agreement to pretend last night didn't happen.

What happens in Vegas stays in Vegas, right?

Well, I think that's bullshit, but I can't tell where Mya stands on this. Are doubts starting to creep in? Is she wishing last night didn't happen?

Maybe a part of me is afraid to find out because I'm hoping our newfound chemistry will continue on our home turf.

After the plane lands, Mya lets out a sigh of relief as the pilot makes his announcement and welcomes us back to the nation's capital.

"We made it. Safe and sound. I told you we had this in the bag."

Her lips curl up slightly. "Things didn't go exactly as planned though, did they?"

I wish I could read her mind right now because her comments aren't giving anything away. That statement could be referencing last night's dinner debacle with the Lavin team or our late-night mattress wrestling. Her expression gives nothing away.

Flying across the country and back within twenty-four hours has even the most perky of our employees looking dead on their feet. Even Kevin is quiet, and he usually doesn't miss an opportunity to talk James's ear off.

"No. But I don't regret any of it," I tell her in a low voice, so we won't be overheard by the others who are walking past, eager to get off this plane and go home.

"I don't regret it either," Mya finally responds.

Relief floods my veins, and it's as refreshing as a rain shower on a hot day. I didn't know just how much it mattered to me until I thought she was having second thoughts.

"So, what do we do now?"

I know exactly what I want to happen. For Mya to

follow me to my place so we can pick up where we left off in Vegas. Mind-blowing sex in a hotel room can only be topped by the comfort of my own bed. But based on her body language and the way her eyes won't meet mine, I'm pretty sure she's not up for a repeat any time soon.

Or ever.

"Milo, I just need some time to think. I don't regret it. Not even slightly," she says with a small smile that assuages my ego somewhat. "But now that we're back, I have to think about what this all means because it doesn't just affect us. James and the whole team are counting on us to pull off a win here. I'm not sure we can afford any distractions right now."

Everything she's saying makes sense. I would love to argue that sex between us wouldn't be a distraction but there's no way in hell I can pretend that's true. Every single thing about Mya Taylor distracts me.

"You're right."

"I am?" Her expression betrays her shock.

"Hey, you're not the only one worried about this blowing up in our faces. I just have two requests. Rules for this new reality, if you will. Number one, we don't let things get weird. It happened, and it was the most amazing night of my life. But if it can never happen again, I understand. We'll keep things professional from here on out."

"The most amazing night of your life, huh?"

I chuckle at her self-satisfied grin. "Yeah, it was."

"For me, too."

My heart shouldn't be beating this fast at her admission. "Number two, that we keep things professional at work. The office is like Switzerland. Neutral ground."

"I completely agree." Mya's eyes meet mine and she looks grateful. "Thank you for understanding. And for... you know. Everything." She blushes as she says it.

Just like that I'm hard as a rock. With just one word, it's like I'm back in that hotel room again, doing the most depraved things I can think of, all to make her shake with pleasure.

Don't make it weird.

Keep it professional.

"Milo? Mya? Are you coming?"

James is waiting at the front of the plane. Everyone else has gone, and we're the only ones left. The flight attendant stands at the head of the aisle waiting.

"Shit, I guess we'd better go before they kick us out."

Mya gathers her things and follows me off the plane. We walk across the tarmac and enter the main terminal. With a wave for James, I follow Mya onto the elevator that will take us to where she parked her car.

We're silent the whole time, having said everything we wanted to say on the plane. But this time it's not a comfortable silence. The air is heavy with all the things I'm holding back.

"This is me." Mya points to her small gray economy car.

"I'm one level down."

We stand awkwardly for a few seconds before she opens her arms for a hug.

Fuck professionalism, I think before sliding my hand up under her low ponytail and pulling her closer. If this is all I can ever have, then I'll take it all. I close my eyes soaking up the sensation of her soft curves pressing against me.

"I'll see you on Monday, beautiful."

With a shaky nod, she climbs into her car, and I watch as she drives off. Then I walk back to the elevators.

We've already violated rule number one because that was definitely weird.

———

OVER THE WEEKEND, I have time to reset my equilibrium. Once I'm away from Mya, it's like the fog clears a little, and I can see how far into the weeds we'd gone.

What was I doing?

I'd finally met a woman who was open to sex with no strings, and here I was pining for more. Mya was basically like a unicorn, that perfect specimen of woman that I'd always hoped I'd find. Beautiful, sexy and independent.

So, what the hell is wrong with me? I should be celebrating. Instead I just have a vaguely sick sense that I've lost something precious.

I hate to admit that she might have been right about this affecting our work. Her behavior when we got back on Friday afternoon leads me to believe things will be awkward in the office. Mya could barely look me in the eye when we hugged goodbye, so how are we going to collaborate effectively on the Lavin campaign? But it's only going down that way if we allow it to.

I arrive in the office early on Monday with my counterattack measures ready to go.

As usual, I'm the first one in, so I have the break room to myself as I brew the coffee. Before I'm done, Anya wanders in.

"Hey, congrats on the Lavin meeting. I heard it went really well."

"Thank you. I think this is going to be one of our biggest projects to date."

I don't bother asking how she heard about it already when everyone who went to Vegas didn't report back to the office after we landed. It was already late in the day and we were all exhausted, so James told us all to go straight home. Anya always seems to know everything that's going on around here. It wouldn't surprise me at all if she knew what happened at dinner Thursday night as it was happening.

Hell, Wallace might have even posted about it on Instagram.

"Anya, does Mya have any meetings first thing this morning?"

She shrugs. "Nothing that I'm aware of. Planning on sneaking into a supply closet with your fiancée?"

It's clear from how she's grinning that she's bought the story and thinks Mya and I have been canoodling at the office this whole time.

Good. That works in my favor.

"Perhaps."

"Well, I won't stop you. Someone needs to have fun around this place." She wiggles her fingers over her shoulder as she walks away.

I leave the door to my office open so I can watch the hallway, which is the only reason I notice when Mya comes in. She marches down the hall with her head held high, not even sparing a glance toward my open office door.

So, it's like that?

I decide to give it another hour, just to be fair. Maybe she has a ton of stuff going on that requires her attention this morning.

Never let it be said that I'm not a patient man.

When another hour passes and Mya doesn't call, text,

email or drop by, I realize that she's definitely violating rule one. We talked everyday even when we were pretending to hate each other. But now she can't even acknowledge that my office door exists?

It stings a little, being ignored, even if I know why she's doing it. But if she thinks pretending I'm not here is going to fix this, then she needs to think again. I wait until I see her walk down the hall, coffee cup in hand, before I make my move.

The hall is empty, so no one sees me slip into Mya's office. I sit in her chair and turn it so it's facing away from the door. It has such a high back that no one will know I'm here unless I turn around.

About ten minutes later I hear the door close, so I turn around in the chair slowly.

Mya squeals. "Milo? What the hell? You almost gave me a heart attack."

"Now you can see me? Oh, that's good. I figured I must be invisible considering that you rushed right past my open door and couldn't see it."

"I was in a hurry," she protests.

"You were being weird, which we agreed not to do."

Her face falls. "You're right. That was weird and rude. I guess I just don't have a lot of experience with this kind of thing."

"Believe it or not, neither do I. Things are awkward, I

get it, but our plan will work if we both commit to it. If we work together, I know we can come up with some kick-ass campaigns that are sure to wow the Lavin team."

"Sounds good to me." She sets her coffee on the edge of the table just as Anya walks in carrying another vase of flowers.

The sight of that obnoxious bouquet causes an unexpected pang in the center of my chest. Before Mya can move, I jump up and take the flowers from Anya bringing them back to the desk.

"Meet me at my place after work," I whisper. "We can work on our campaigns. I'll text you the address."

Then my eyes stray to the flowers in the corner again.

"And have a bonfire."

Before she can overthink it, I lift her chin and plant a soft kiss on her lips. Anya gives me a thumbs-up before she backs out of the room.

"You shouldn't have done that. Anya is the biggest gossip in the office. They'll all be talking about us before lunch."

She says it as if that should frighten me but truthfully, I don't care if the whole office is gossiping about us. Whatever they're saying isn't going to come anywhere near the actual truth.

"Let them talk."

MYA

BY THE TIME the end of the day rolls around, my eyes are burning from staring at my computer screen. I've been working on my design ideas for the Lavin campaign all day, but so far nothing I've come up with is good enough.

My eyes stray to the clock in the upper right corner of my monitor. Milo is expecting me to come over tonight to work on our campaigns together.

In theory that sounds like a good idea, but then when you break it down, I have to remember that he is still my competition. Our ideas are going to go head-to-head, and Mr. Lavin can only pick one of them. So why should I give up my ideas to him ahead of time?

We've built a temporary trust between us but I'm still not ready to put all my eggs in that basket. It's better if I develop my ideas independently so there can be no misunderstandings later.

Mr. Lavin is going to love what I come up with. And I don't want anyone else trying to take credit for my ideas.

James pokes his head in from the hall. "How are things going?"

"Great. The research we did before the meeting has been useful. I've come up with several possible directions we could take for a bridal campaign."

"Fantastic. I haven't heard anything else yet, but once Mr. Lavin is ready to move on this, I'd like to be able to accommodate his schedule."

Which is a subtle warning to get it together in case the client asks for a meeting out of the blue. No pressure or anything.

My phone blares the raunchy lyrics to Big Sean's *I Don't Fuck With You,* and we both pause in shock. I grab my bag and stick my hand inside, hoping and praying that for once I'll find my phone quickly amidst all the junk in there.

I Don't Fuck With YOU. The volume is even louder now that I'm holding my bag open.

James coughs slightly. "Right, I'll check back in with you later. I have a meeting." He's trying to talk over the sound of the music but it's nearly impossible.

"No problem, boss. I'll put together a draft campaign for you to review by the end of the week."

I Don't Fuck... my face flames as I continue to rummage through my bag... *with YOU.*

James is still smiling when he walks away.

My office door is wide open, and one of the interns from Kevin's department scampers away when I look up.

Damn Ariana and her crazy ringtones!

Every time I leave my phone around her, she programs in whatever song captures her current feelings. I guess she was feeling nihilistic last time. By the time I find my phone the ringtone has finally stopped.

ARIANA SILVA

Drop whatever you're doing. I'm off work early and in the mood for margaritas.

It's not like Ariana to get off work early or to text me about it. Which means that she had a really shitty day. She's a pediatric nurse, so her bad days are really bad. If she lost a patient, then I definitely don't want her to be alone. The thing about Ari is that she'll never admit when she needs someone.

MYA TAYLOR

K, on my way. I'll take the metro and come to you.

I turn off my computer and grab my bag and coat. It's not like I was getting anything done anyway. Maybe a margarita is exactly what I need to cut loose.

Twenty minutes later I'm getting off the metro at the Foggy Bottom station. As soon as I come up the escalator I see Ariana waiting. Her face looks pinched and tired, and she hasn't changed out of her scrubs yet. Things are definitely bad if she wants to go out for drinks without changing first.

As I approach I hold out my arms, and she accepts the hug.

"Hey girl. Thanks for coming. I should have known you could decode my bat signal." She hooks her arm through mine and leads me through the throngs of people clustered around the escalators leading to the metro below ground. I follow her lead, assuming she knows where she's going. This is her turf not mine.

"It was the getting off work early part that gave you away. Your boss never lets you off early."

"Technically she didn't let me off early this time either. It was the attending physician who told me to take off."

She pulls me through a doorway, and I look around the dark interior of the restaurant.

Ari takes a seat at the bar. "I've heard this place has the best tapas in the city and their margaritas are so strong that just one will have you spilling your secrets."

She points to the menu on the bar and orders two strawberry margaritas. Soon, we're both sucking down the sweet liquid and it feels like all my stress is just melting away.

Ariana sighs. "Today was a rough one. I'm not sure if this is the right fit for me. It takes a really thick skin to see all this suffering and not be affected by it."

"You're a great nurse, Ari. As crazy as you are, you have the biggest, squishiest heart. Those babies are lucky to have someone like you to take care of them. Especially the ones whose parents can't be there."

Ari volunteers her time in the neonatal unit when she's off shift to hold and snuggle the babies whose parents can't visit as often. Some of them live too far to get to the NICU often, and others have to work so hard just to afford the medical bills. Ariana comes in and fills the gap, so those babies have someone there for them.

"Enough about me and my bad day. I want to hear all about you and Happy Hour Hottie. You've been so quiet all weekend. You never even told me how the trip went."

"The trip was great." I smile brightly, but I should have known that wouldn't fool her. Ariana can smell drama from a mile away.

She gasps. "Did you actually take my advice and have a little fun?"

It's weird to talk about this because I don't even know

what Milo and I are doing. We're fake engaged at work, but we're also supposed to be keeping things professional. This mental yo-yo is taking a toll, and we've only been back at work for one day.

"The meeting with the client was a disaster."

Ari sucks down the last of her margarita as I recount the whole tale. By the time I reach the end, she waves her hand at me to continue.

"That's it. We lied, and now the entire office is gossiping about us."

I decide to leave out the part about Milo pledging to show me what good sex is supposed to be like.

"Girl, some shit going down with your job is NOT why you've been whistling a happy tune since you came back. Either you found your own Magic Mike while you were down there, or you did the nasty with Happy Hour Hottie. So, which is it?"

I lose my grip on my margarita glass and almost spill what's left. "Damn! Is it that obvious?"

"Um, do you really want me to answer that?"

Glumly, I stare into the remains of my drink. "How did this whole thing get so complicated? Everything was going wrong and then I ended up in his hotel room. And then everything was going *right*. Now I'm not sure what's up with us. It was so awkward seeing him today."

"Look, I know you won't listen to my advice but there's nothing wrong with having a little fun with your sexy coworker. You're both adults, and no one is getting hurt. It sounds like you've both been honest about what you want from this. You got your heart broken, and now you're just having a little fun. Hot, sweaty sex is the cure for heartbreak."

The bartender chooses that exact moment to come back and check on us. He grins at Ariana's words.

She points at him with one red-lacquered nail. "Don't you agree that hot sex is the best cure when you get your heart broken?"

He takes one look at her almost-empty margarita glass and immediately starts making her another one. "I think that would cure just about anything, sweetheart."

Ari looks at me with an *I told you so* face. "See? Big, muscly bartender man agrees with me."

I resist the urge to roll my eyes. Because of course taking sex advice from a random guy in a bar sounds like a good idea.

"But this is not me. I don't do stuff like this."

"Did you enjoy yourself?"

I can feel my cheeks heating. "Definitely. That man is a beast in bed."

Ari holds her margarita aloft like a trophy. "Yes! I knew it. My girl finally got it right."

Her words settle over me, and I roll them around my brain.

Did I get it right?

Ari is always saying I need to stop overthinking everything and just have some fun. That's never been easy for me. Ever since I was a kid, I've always liked to have things planned out and organized. A list of goals for every area of my life.

But I had a checklist that included finding the perfect guy and getting married, and look how that turned out.

According to all my lists and rules, Milo is the last person that I should spend time with. He's impulsive and reckless, allergic to commitment, and just out for a good time.

But you know what? I never had as much fun with 'perfect' William as I did with Milo.

Not just the great sex but everything. Even just talking to him was more fun than I've had in a long time.

Which scares the hell out of me.

"You know what? You're absolutely right," I announce, pushing my now empty margarita glass down the bar.

Ariana pauses with her straw halfway to her mouth. "I am?"

"Yes. I do need to get out there and have some fun. I definitely need to stop worrying about what the men in my life want and start thinking about what I want."

That includes Milo. What the hell does he think he's doing kissing me and telling me to come to his place after work? He's a pro at this casual sex thing and leaving emotion out of it is probably second nature for him.

Well, it's not that easy for me. I have to take care of my own needs from now on. And getting attached to Milo in any way is not a smart move.

If William had the power to hurt me, someone like Milo could crush my heart into a million pieces.

"So what are you going to do?" Ari asks.

"I'm going to have some fun. And another margarita." I raise my finger signaling the bartender for another drink.

fifteen

MILO

I'M at home in the middle of changing clothes when my phone lights up with a text from Mya. All afternoon, I've been waiting to get a text or email that she's changed her mind and isn't coming over. It's expected. This is new territory for both of us, and Mya looked pretty freaked out earlier today.

But when I open the text, I have to read it three times before it makes sense.

A startled laugh escapes. Maybe I misread her mood earlier. She doesn't sound pissed off at all. And she's calling me a hottie.

MYA TAYLOR

Mya's having fun, but can't get her off the bar. She's had about fvh% margaritas 2 many.

My brow furrows as I scan the message again. Did she mean to send this text to someone else?

But no, why would she send someone a text about herself having too many margaritas? Then another text comes in.

MYA TAYLOR

Oops, this is Mya's roommate. I've had a few myself.

Ah, now it's starting to make sense. But my relief disappears when I realize what it means for Mya's roommate to have her phone.

MILO HAMILTON

Why is she on the bar?

MYA TAYLOR

Dancing! There's a lot of guys here and

The message just stops. I'm staring at it for a few seconds before I realize no more is coming.

Shit.

Her roommate probably isn't in any better shape than she is judging from these messages.

It's none of your business, I remind myself.

Mya clearly didn't want to see me tonight, otherwise she would have come over instead of going out drinking. Then I imagine Mya drunk and vulnerable in a bar full of guys.

I grab a sweatshirt from my closet and pull it on.

MILO HAMILTON

Tell me where you are.

Five minutes later I have the address. It's going to be hell to find parking this time of day, so I call for an Uber. The entire way there, I tell myself that I'm not being creepy by checking up on Mya.

Clearly she meant to blow me off tonight and just not come over or call, but that doesn't mean I want her to be in an unsafe situation. I've never seen her drink a lot at the office happy hour events, so something tells me this is not her usual behavior.

I definitely don't want her or her roommate walking alone if they're intoxicated.

The tapas bar is in Foggy Bottom, not far from George Washington University Hospital. It's a nice area with a lot of new development, but you really can't be too careful in the city.

Like I suspected, traffic is crazy. When we get stuck behind a stalled car, I tell the Uber driver that I'll just hop out and walk the rest of the way. The bar is only about a block away, and I hear the music before I get there. When I open the door, I scan the crowd looking for Mya. But before I get too far, someone grabs my arm.

A stunning woman wearing nurse's scrubs leans way too close. "There you are, Happy Hour Hottie!"

This must be the roommate. She called me that in her text message, too. I have a feeling there's a story there, and I'm going to enjoy tormenting Mya until she admits who came up with that name.

"In the flesh. And you are?"

She holds out her hand. "Ariana Silva. I guess I should have introduced myself when I texted you, but I've kind of had my hands full here."

"Where is Mya? Is she okay?"

She points behind me and I turn to see Mya dancing near the end of the bar. She's still wearing the conservative blouse and skirt she wore to work today, but she's unbuttoned more than a few buttons on her blouse so an alarming amount of cleavage is on display. Her high heels lay abandoned on the floor a few feet away while two guys dance around her. One of them is practically dry humping her from behind.

My mouth falls open.

Ariana looks sheepish. "At least I got her off the bar. I didn't realize how many drinks she'd had until she took her shoes off. Then those guys showed up. I mean I'm no cock-block, but she didn't even protest when I asked for her phone. She's in no shape to go home with some random guy."

"But you called me. Why?" Not that I'm complaining but from her roommate's perspective, I'm just a random guy, too.

"You're her fiancé, aren't you?" Ariana winks.

"I guess that means she told you about Vegas."

I'm not sure I want to know what she told her friend about our trip. It also doesn't seem like a good sign that instead of coming over Mya went out with her friend and got trashed.

"She told me, but I also know that you two used to be friends. You can tell a lot about a man by how he responds when you need him. You're a good guy, Triple H."

Her cheeky response makes me smile. "You think so?"

Ariana sways slightly, confirming my suspicion that she's not in much better shape than Mya. "You're here, aren't you? Mya needed you, and you showed up. That's all I need to know. And on that note, I'm going to take an Uber home. I'll let you figure out how to get Mya out of here."

I laugh at her bold personality. She's not who I would have thought would be friends with Mya, but I can see why they work together. Someone like Ariana is exactly what Mya needs in her life to help her have fun.

Something you won't be helping her with anymore, clearly.

I ignore the bitter part of me that wishes things had turned out differently. But no matter what, Ariana is right. We were friends. Hell, we are friends even if Mya doesn't want to be. I'll always think of her as a friend.

Mya doesn't even notice when I approach, but the guys dancing with her do. I give them both my best menacing stare.

The one dancing in front of her leaves immediately and tries to get his friend to leave too, but the other guy shakes his head.

"What's your problem, man? Get your own girl." His eyes are glassy, and his cheeks start to go red.

The bartender walks our way, probably anticipating a fight.

"I am getting my girl. You're dancing with her. That's my fiancée you're grinding on."

Mya looks up at that. "Milo? What are you doing here?"

All of a sudden, it's as if she notices the guy pushing up behind her. Her nose wrinkles, and then she covers her cheeks with her hands.

"Uh oh, I'm in trouble."

The guy looks between us in alarm and then holds up his hands. "I didn't know she had a husband!"

Mya giggles uncontrollably. "He's not my husband. Nobody wants to be my husband."

Oh boy. It's definitely time to get her out of here.

"Time to go, beautiful." I lean down and grab her shoes off the floor. "Where's your stuff?"

Mya pouts when the guy who was dancing with her walks away. "I don't even know his name, but he seemed like fun. William didn't think I was *fun*. He said I was all about work. Work, work, work."

I loop her arm around my neck. "Do you need to close your tab?"

She shakes her head. "No, I paid earlier. Those guys just kept buying me drinks."

"Yeah, I bet they did," I mutter under my breath. "Come on, beautiful. Time to go home."

Now up until this point, I was wondering why Ariana bothered to call me. From the text messages, I was expecting Mya to be three sheets to the wind and singing show tunes at the top of her lungs, but she's been docile as a lamb so far. Getting her home should be a piece of cake.

But apparently, I just mentioned the magic word.

"*Home?* No, I am not going home!" Mya shouts, suddenly wide awake. "Where's Ariana? We're supposed to be having fun!"

One of her hands lands in my face as she practically climbs me trying to get back to the bar.

"Mya, baby. Come on." I grunt as her other hand punches me in the stomach. "Ariana is already at home. Let's go see her."

Mya starts shaking her head back and forth so wildly that she loses her balance. I manage to catch her before she clips the bar, and we both land sprawled on the bar stool.

"No, I don't want to see her at home. That's *boring*. I'm tired of being *booooring*. I'm having drinks, and then I am going to have some meaningless sex!"

Her voice is so loud that it carries even over the music.

A guy across the room yells out, "I'd be happy to help you with that, *mamacita*!" which ignites a round of spirited laughter from the crowd surrounding us.

I close my eyes. "Mya, you are going to seriously owe me for this one. But if you don't come with me, I *will* carry your sexy little ass out of here."

She leans closer, eyes narrowed. "You wouldn't dare."

I bend at the knees and then hoist her over my shoulder in a fireman's hold. Her handbag is on the floor, and I'm trying to figure out how to grab it when the bartender comes from behind the bar and gets it for me.

"Good luck with that one, dude. She's a wildcat."

Mya's nails dig into my lower back. I'm holding her too tightly for her to kick but I guess she figures that she can take her revenge elsewhere.

I wince. "Yeah, she is. But I wouldn't have it any other way."

———

NOW, I'm not saying that you should get an award for doing the right things in life. If something is the right thing to do, you should do it even if no one is watching. That's just the way it is.

But if there ever *were* awards for being a nice guy, I should receive one for this cab ride.

"I can't believe you spanked my ass in front of all of those people!" Mya shrieks, her face half-buried in my shirt.

Hopefully the cab driver isn't paying attention to what we're doing back here because Mya keeps climbing into my lap.

I've tried putting her back on her side of the cab three times, and she always ends up back here with her face buried in my shoulders and her soft round ass rubbing all over my cock. But I'm not touching her at all. She's drunk and emotional right now, and I would never take advantage of that.

Even when she's literally climbing all over me.

Lots of guys would argue that there's nothing wrong with enjoying these incidental touches, but I don't feel right getting hot and bothered when I'm not sure Mya knows what she's doing. So every time she climbs on my lap, I deposit her gently back in her seat.

See what I mean? Award material, right there.

"I only spanked your ass because you were scratching me. That hurt, and I needed to get you out of that bar before you invited one of those guys home with us."

We're stuck in traffic, so I'm contemplating whether I should put her back on her side of the cab again or just give in and let her stay where she is since she's calming down now. But then I feel something ticklish moving over my lips. Mya is tracing my face with her fingertips.

"You're so sweet to me," she says. Her eyes close like she's too tired to keep them open, but she's still mumbling to herself. "I wish you weren't. It was so much easier to hate you when you weren't being so nice."

Her voice is mournful, and it makes me want to take care of her. I don't like hearing her sound like this.

"Of course I'm nice to you, Mya. You're my–" I falter, not sure what to call her. But she shushes me, holding a finger to my mouth.

"Don't say it. It's supposed to be a secret."

Now I'm confused. I'm not sure if she's talking about us or something else. "What's supposed to be a secret?" But she doesn't answer, so I stroke her hair and say, "Sleep, Mya. We'll be home soon."

She sighs, and the sound carries such sadness. "I'm

going home alone. He didn't want to keep me, you know? William didn't want to keep me. So now I'm alone. Always alone."

The longing in her voice calls out to me. Because the way she looks right now is the way I've felt so many times alone in the city. Mya is right to have concerns about us. About where this is going and about how we'll function at work because of it.

But right now, none of that matters. There's no work, there's no client, there's no Mirage.

There's just two lonely people in a cab.

I lean forward and tap lightly on the plexiglass separating us from the cab driver. "Sorry, change of plans."

Maybe I'll regret this later, but right now I don't care. I can't fix everything for Mya, but I can fix this. Neither of us has to be lonely tonight.

I give the cab driver my address.

sixteen

MYA

THIS PILLOW IS the softest thing I've ever had my face smashed into.

You wouldn't think that would be the telltale sign that clues me in that I'm not at home, but as I burrow my face deeper into the silky fabric, all I'm thinking is *these are not the bargain sheets I bought at Walmart.*

I tentatively open one eye and am rewarded with a brass band playing right in the center of my skull.

"Have mercy." I clutch my head with both hands and attempt to retreat back under the covers. But I can't escape the thing that woke me.

Is that bacon?

The sweet smell convinces me that leaving the cocoon of the covers is worth it. I'm willing to brave the unknown for bacon.

I sit up gingerly holding my head. What did I do last night? I'm currently occupying a massive bed amidst a jumble of pillows. The predominant colors are navy blue accented with silver. Aside from the pile of pillows and linens next to me, it's clean and ruthlessly organized.

When I close my eyes, I get a flash of memory, my arms around Milo's neck as he placed me on the bed.

This is Milo's room.

I'm in his bed.

Which means he saw you drunk and out of control last night.

Great.

As embarrassing as this is, I'm not going to hide in the bedroom all day. It's a workday so I have to get it together. I swing my legs over the side of the bed and stand carefully. The room swirls for a moment and then comes into focus.

How much did I have to drink last night?

Bits and pieces float through my memory but nothing concrete. Ariana figures prominently in the memories I do have so I decide this situation is entirely her fault. Especially since the only way I could have ended up with Milo is if she called him. There's no way he'd have known where we were otherwise.

I shake my head. The girl has balls. She wouldn't have called him if she hadn't known I'd be completely safe with him but still. After hearing what happened in Vegas, she's got all her money on Team Milo, no matter how many times I tell her this is just a temporary thing. This is her way of pushing the issue.

Then I'm hit with another memory of being sprawled over his lap in the cab. My head falls forward. I'm going to have to face him after I practically humped his leg on the way here.

I'm wearing only my bra and panties, so he must have undressed me before leaving me to sleep. There's a sweatshirt at the foot of the bed, so I pull that on and then venture out to find the source of that amazing smell.

Milo's back is to me when I enter the kitchen, so I take a moment to admire a truly spectacular ass covered in black boxer-briefs.

How the hell did he hide *that ass* under those tailored suits all this time?

I was probably too distracted by the rest of him to notice, but now that it's on display and waggling in my face, I'm going to enjoy the view. I stifle a giggle when the music blaring from his phone registers.

"Does Wallace know you're a Justin Bieber fan?" My smile widens when his ass pauses mid-hip thrust at my words.

He glances over his shoulder. "You have a light step. I didn't know you were there." He reaches over and turns the music down. "And my love of pop music is going to stay between you and me. If anything, that would just make Wallace decide that we need to be friends."

After turning off the burner under whatever he's cooking, Milo walks over to me. Actually, *walking* is probably a mild word for how he stalks over, all rolling hips and intense eyes. He plants his hands on either side of me and then proceeds to kiss every thought from my head.

By the time he pulls back, we're both breathing hard and his cock is trying to work its way out of the waistband of his underwear.

"Good morning," he murmurs before turning back to the counter where there's a plate of bacon and a stack of pancakes.

"Damn right it is," I mumble as I take a seat.

Over breakfast we talk about everything other than my drunken escapade the night before. I'm grateful for the reprieve and that he doesn't mention that I ditched him after work. Now that I'm looking back on it, I'm ashamed of how I handled things yesterday.

Yes, it's weird to work alongside someone that you have insane sexual chemistry with. But Milo has done everything he can to make me feel comfortable and respected.

He's been a perfect gentleman.

I've been a jerk.

"Thank you for coming to get me from the bar. I didn't know Ari was going to call you, but I'm glad she did."

Milo kisses me on the forehead. "It was my pleasure. I wouldn't have missed that show for the world. Especially the part where you announced to the whole bar that you wanted to have some meaningless sex."

Groaning, I cover my face. "I've obviously mentally blocked some of this out. Please tell me there's no video evidence of that."

He chuckles. "If only I'd known to have my phone out. There's no telling if someone else got it though. You'd just better hope no one puts it on YouTube."

We both laugh at that. I help him collect our plates from the table, and it's a comfortable silence as we work side-by-side to clean up.

"You know I didn't mind coming to get you, right?" Milo is watching me with an inscrutable expression on his face.

After everything that's happened between us the last few days, I'm not really sure what to make of it. Other than that scorching kiss this morning, he's been sweet but distant. Not that I can blame him after last night. I was a hot mess.

"I do know that. You're a good friend to me, Milo. I'm ashamed to say that I didn't think you would be, but obviously I'm a terrible judge of character. The man I thought would always be there for me, left without a backward glance. And the guy I thought I hated, well, he's turned out to be the one I can count on."

He's still watching me with that intense gaze. Then his

eyes lower to my lips. "You deserve a man who'll do those things, Mya. Isn't that what I promised to show you?"

My mouth goes dry. "You promised to teach me a lot of things. But I'm not really sure I got the lesson the first time."

His eyes heat at my words. "Is that right? Maybe you need some reinforcement? Another lesson. Or two? Hell, I still feel like I need to get you to three or four. Multiples should be a given."

Then he picks me up and carries me back down the hall toward the bedroom.

Oh my.

I gulp when Milo places me gently on his massive king-size bed amidst the jumbled bed linen. *Holy mother.* Suddenly, things are happening so fast, and Milo is looking at me strangely, with a tender expression that makes me wish this was more than just two people with a killer case of lust.

It makes me wish I was the woman he loved.

"If you've changed your mind I won't hold it against you. I don't want to do anything you don't want to do." Milo peers down at me, his eyes narrowed with concern, obviously interpreting my silence as second thoughts.

I trail my fingers over the hard muscles of his chest, counting the freckles scattered across his collarbone. I lean over to press a kiss against the taut skin of his lower belly and he gasps, the sound loud in the quiet room.

"I haven't changed my mind. Have you?" I yank the sweatshirt I borrowed over my head.

He locks his hand in my hair and tugs firmly until I look up at him. "Sometimes I think you have no idea just what you do to me."

Before I have the chance to process his words, his mouth is on mine, hot and insistent. He keeps the contact even as he stretches out on the bed beside me, as if unwilling to separate for even that short length of time. He kisses the same way he does everything, with intensity. His hands skim over my curves before they stop on my ass.

He makes his way down my neck, gently sucking the soft skin where my throat meets my collarbone as he rotates his hips in a slow, grinding rhythm.

My hands slip over the damp skin of his back as I rock my hips to help him hit just the right spot.

"Milo, please. Please help me."

I push at the waistband of his boxers, trying to force the material over his hips. Milo sits back just long enough to take them off. His cock stands away from his body, long and thick, the head so engorged with blood it looks red.

My pussy clenches, remembering the last time I was stretched full of that.

Damn.

He reaches for me, but I shake my head and push him

on his back. His cock bobs between us as if begging for attention. Attention I'm more than happy to provide.

"What's the matter?" He raises his eyebrows, and I hold up a hand to cut him off.

"A view like this requires some reflection." I lean down until his thick flesh is so close it touches my nose. "I need a moment of silence."

I wrap my hand around his cock, and he sucks in a sudden breath.

"By all means, pay your respects."

He watches intently as I brush my lips lightly over the whole length. His skin is soft, like silk over steel. When I reach the mushroom-shaped tip, I circle the head with my tongue, reveling in the musky flavor. Sucking his cock factored heavily in my sweaty, forbidden dreams of him, so I close my eyes and do what I've been imagining for so long.

Swallow the whole length.

"Holy fuck! Mya, goddamn." His voice is an awed whisper as he watches me take his cock all the way to the back of my throat.

I take my time, drawing him between my lips slowly, testing his control. His breath falters when I tug lightly at the tip, which heightens my own arousal. I love that I can bring him to this state, sweating and groaning until he's hoarse.

When I hollow my cheeks and suck hard, he barks out a harsh cry and grabs my hair.

"*Jesus*, woman. The things you can do with that mouth."

I still with my lips playing over the soft skin of his shaft and look up at him teasingly. He growls in warning, his hands tightening in my hair almost to the point of pain.

"I can't take any more, or things will be over before they start." He withdraws gently and then leans over and grabs a condom from the nightstand.

Suddenly shy again, I bury my face in the pillow. He brushes my hair back and kisses my forehead, my nose, my cheeks. He continues his erotic journey, his lips skimming over my breastbone and belly. Our eyes meet right before his tongue darts out, lashing my clit. I cry out, unable to hold back.

He takes another taste, a longer, deeper lick I feel clear to my toes. I shudder as he delves deeper, the slight stubble on his face adding another dimension to the sensation.

"You are so beautiful." His voice is rough as he settles on top of me again.

Finally.

"Now, where were we? Oh yes, working on making you beg."

He rubs his cock against my slit, my cream coating him with each pass. I arch my back, trying to force him inside, but he chuckles as his hips keep working, slowly driving me to insanity.

"Milo, for god's sake. Please."

"Say it. I want to hear you say it." He rests his damp forehead against mine and looks down into my eyes.

His pupils have dilated so much his eyes look black. I shiver as he increases the friction. He swallows my gasps of pleasure as he sips at my mouth, his dark gaze locked on mine, begging for words I'm not sure I can say. My senses are on overload from all the different sensations, the tickle of his chest against my nipples, the moisture on our bodies as we writhe against each other.

"I need you inside me." My voice breaks as he surges inside in a sudden, thick thrust.

He's so large I'm stretched almost to the point of pain, and the sharp pressure fills me with a dark ache. His eyes are open and locked on mine. I couldn't look away even if I wanted to.

"You're mine, Mya." He rides me hard, his hands holding my hips as the tip of his cock drags over my G-spot.

I undulate on the bed, my inner muscles squeezing him involuntarily. He clenches his jaw, his thrusts quickening. I shiver when his forehead drops to my chest and he licks the damp moisture between my breasts away. When he turns his head, the hot wash of his breath heats my skin right before his mouth latches on to my nipple. I squeeze my eyes shut and surrender to the hot, wet pressure.

"You're so fucking tight, I can't take it," he growls, his voice ragged.

The veins in his neck and arms stand out sharply against his olive skin as he lifts my legs up and over his shoulders, the new position forcing him deeper. The base of his cock pounds against my clit with every stroke.

It's amazingly erotic, the sight of his tight muscles shifting, the wet sound of our skin slapping together, the cries we can't hold back. It's all too much, and I scream as my orgasm bursts through me in a blinding explosion. My pussy clamps down so hard even Milo jolts at the pleasure-pain. He continues to move through the clenching spasms, stroking me into a second smaller orgasm.

"You feel so good. You're so wet." He moans against my neck as he gives in to his own release.

We stay just like that for a few minutes, both of us too exhausted to move. Finally, he throws a heavy arm over my middle and pulls me back until I'm nestled against him. Being so close to him, cuddled together warm under the covers, is somehow even more intimate than what we just did.

And it feels just as right.

seventeen

MILO

I'M WALKING BACK to my room when there's a knock at the door. Assuming Mya left something behind, I double back and yank the door open.

"Did you forget–" My voice dies when I see Ethan standing there.

"I didn't forget anything. But I guess this means you forgot that we have a meeting this morning?"

"Fuck." I walk away leaving the front door open. "Give me ten minutes."

"Was that Mya I just saw leaving?" Ethan yells at my back.

"If you're here to give me another lecture about corporate policy or whatever, you can fuck off."

The sound of his laughter follows me into my room. The front door slams. Apparently giving me a lecture isn't worth losing the opportunity to ride my ass, one of his favorite pastimes.

"I'm not here to give you a lecture. When has speaking sense ever worked with you?"

"Good point. So why are you here? We usually meet at the office." I grab the first suit my hand lands on. Then I select a tie to match.

Ethan leans against the door jamb. "Call me crazy, but I thought you might need a friend. There's been a lot going on lately."

It's hard to admit, but I am glad to see him. Waking up with Mya was intense and not at all what I thought it would be. We're doing this dance, but neither of us knows the steps. She's slowly becoming integral to my life, but neither of us has put a label on it.

Normally that's exactly what I would like. No labels. No strings. No commitment.

But that's not what I want with Mya. I want strings. Hell, I want to tie her up in them so she can never get away.

That doesn't sound right but you know what I mean. Tie her up in a loving way.

Loving bondage?

Jesus, now I even sound creepy in my thoughts.

This whole time Ethan has been watching me. "Damn, you really have it bad, dude."

Somehow this is more embarrassing than calling him in the middle of the night while watching Mya sleep.

"I didn't say anything," I protest.

"You didn't have to," he responds without missing a beat. "It's written all over your dumb face."

"Why do I talk to you again?"

"Because you need someone to tell you the truth. So as the resident asshole in your life, I guess it falls to me to tell you you're fucking up. You work together. What happens when this runs its course?"

I think he expects me to joke back. This is how we relate to each other, jokes and insults, mixed in with useful advice and camaraderie.

But this time I don't feel like joking around. This is not a new experience, having Ethan come over right after some chick leaves.

Watching Mya walk out the door... it was different.

Because she's the only one I've ever wanted to stay.

"I don't think that's going to happen, E. For the first time, I'm not the one running away."

His face betrays his surprise. We've been friends ever since I got hired at Mirage. I get the sense that he doesn't let many people in. Neither do I. But he's one of the few people who knows about what happened with Tessa. I don't normally like to talk about it, but after too many beers one night, the whole story came tumbling out.

Surprisingly he's a very good listener. I get the sense that he's been hurt in his past, too.

"Well, hell. You know I think Mya is fantastic."

"Yeah, she is. Beautiful, smart, and not afraid to hand me my ass."

Ethan shakes his head. "Never thought I'd see the day, but maybe you've done it. Maybe you've found the one."

Somehow hearing him say it out loud makes it sound ridiculous, and that makes me angry. I don't want to fast-forward to thinking about when this all ends.

Maybe I just want five fucking seconds to live in a world where a guy like me deserves a girl like her.

As if he knows what I'm thinking, Ethan tugs at his tie. "Not every girl is like Tessa. Mya seems genuine, like the type who'll stick."

I want to believe that more than I can express. But wishing for things won't make them real. And putting my feelings out there won't make Mya feel the same.

"Make yourself at home. I just need to jump in the shower."

Ethan looks like he wants to say something else but just knocks on the wall. "Take your time. I need your pretty mug to convince the client to sign."

"Is that why you take me to these meetings?"

He points at his scowling expression. "There's a reason

I'm a lawyer. You think *this* is going to convince anybody to part with their money?"

Now I know he's joking because he's a good-looking guy and since he's a partner in his own law firm, wealthy too. He's basically where I want to be in life.

"Ethan, do you really think the forever thing is even possible?" I'm not sure what comes over me, but I suddenly want his take on it.

"I thought I'd found it once. I can relate to this situation more than you know. I was her boss. She was the only one who would take my shit and give it back just as good. But in the end, her heart belonged to someone else. And things weren't the same after she left. That's part of the reason I left Virginia and opened a new location in DC. I needed to get away."

Then he sighs. "I'm the wrong person to ask, man. You should never ask a lawyer to comment on the human condition. We see people at their worst."

It's a measured answer and a mature one. But it's the look on his face that tells me how he really feels. He thinks getting involved is a mistake.

He's a smart guy, one I respect highly. He's got his shit together. If a guy like him can't make a relationship work, then what the fuck am I doing?

———

THE NEXT TWO weeks are intense. Mya and I focus on the project, holing up in my office to work on the campaigns. Our other clients have been handed off until the Lavin presentation is finished. We don't take off early, we work through lunch, and each night we stay longer and longer.

But I didn't mind the long hours because they gave me an excuse to be with Mya all day.

She's funny, impatient as hell, and loves to play devil's advocate. We bicker, tease, and push each other to discover new strengths while also compensating for each other's weaknesses.

I'm exhausted, but I've also never had so much fun.

To reduce the chance for leaks, James has asked us not to use any of the interns or junior associates. So Mya and I have done all the research ourselves and created our visual aids and graphics on our own. Not that I mind, it's actually kind of fun to go back to the grunt work.

In the beginning I thought he was just being paranoid, but once the news about Lavin Bridal is announced, the fashion world goes mad. All my industry contacts are salivating for news on who has the account. We've made it past the first round, but we're well aware that Andre Lavin has plenty of options when it comes to marketing.

We have one chance to impress him. If we screw it up, this chance won't come again.

"I think we've finally got it," Mya says on Friday afternoon.

Making an executive decision, I lean over and save the presentation on her computer and then log off.

"Come on. We're getting out of here."

"What? No, no. *We have so much work to do.*"

But I'm already pulling her to her feet. "We've done as much as we can do. Both of our campaigns are ready. We've practiced how to present them and done several run throughs. Now we need to get out of here because I think this chair is starting to form a permanent mold of my ass."

Her eyes sparkle as she peers behind me playfully. "Really? Well, it is a pretty spectacular ass, I have to say."

"Don't let Ethan hear you say that. Otherwise you'll be getting the sexual harassment lecture, too."

She's laughing at me, but at least she's moving. We've put in the work and done our research. I don't think either of us is really worried about the quality of our work. There's a certain point where you just have to trust that you've done all you can do, and then you have to let the work stand for itself.

Mya shrugs into her coat and grabs her bag from the floor by her desk. "Not sure why I feel guilty for leaving at five when we've been practically sleeping here this week."

"Whenever Mr. Lavin has time in his schedule, we'll be ready for him. That's all that anyone can ask of us."

Anya waves goodbye as we pass her desk, and after a short elevator ride, we escape the confines of the office.

"Fresh air! How long has it been?" Mya spins around in a circle before collapsing against my chest with a giggle.

"Too long. I think we were both starting to get a little punch-drunk after being in that building for so many hours each day. Your place?"

We've fallen into the routine of spending our evenings together lately too. I have to admit that I do prefer my place simply because it's bigger and I can lay her naked on any surface without worrying about a roommate interrupting or overhearing.

Ariana teases us about being loud and makes a show of putting her headphones on whenever I show up now, which is funny, but I know Mya finds it kind of embarrassing. Her relationship with Ariana seems to be more like that of a sibling than just a roommate.

When I heard Ari refer to Mya's ex-boyfriend as the "bad-sex-ex" I knew we would be friends.

"Yeah. I need to do laundry. But maybe we can go to your place tomorrow. It's nice to be alone." She hooks her arm through mine as we walk over to my car.

"You just like my huge bed," I tease.

She likes to take all her clothes off and roll around in my sheets. It smells like her for days.

I love it.

Twenty minutes later, we're parked outside her building. It always takes a while to find a space in her neighborhood, one of the reasons Mya doesn't own a car. Having a car in the city is a pain and expensive, but I like having the freedom to go visit my mom and my brother whenever I want, so I pay the exorbitant price for parking in my building.

"You know what, I think I'll just change my clothes and then we can go to your place after all. After this week, I think we both need some peace and quiet."

I nod in agreement. As much fun as Ariana can be, quiet she is not.

Mya opens the door, and I follow her inside. An older woman looks up from the pot she's stirring at the stove.

"Baby! You're home!" The older woman bustles from behind the counter and holds her arms open to Mya. Then she turns to me, a speculative gleam in her warm brown eyes. "And who is this handsome man?"

Mya turns to me with an apologetic smile. "Mom, this is Milo. He's my... he's my..."

"I'm her boyfriend. It's wonderful to meet you, Mrs. Taylor." I extend my hand and am immediately yanked into a bone-crushing hug.

Over her mom's shoulder, I see Mya wringing her hands and hopping from foot to foot.

Mrs. Taylor finally releases me with a soft exclamation.

"Call me Martine, please. Oh, I need to turn the stew down. Mya, don't leave that nice boy in the doorway! Invite him in. Your father will be back any minute. He went to the store to get some more milk."

"I'm so sorry about this," Mya whispers. "You can go if you want. I'll catch up with you later. My parents like to drop by sometimes out of the blue."

"Leave? You think I'm giving up this opportunity to find out more about pre-ballbuster Mya? Not a chance." I close the door behind me and hang my coat by the door.

When I turn around, Mya is watching me, her face both hopeful and wary. I don't think she knows how easily her face expresses her emotions, but honestly, I hope she never stops giving me these little glimpses into what she's thinking and feeling.

Because I may not know where this thing between us is going, but I know I haven't had nearly enough of her yet.

Not even close.

MYA

SEVERAL HOURS later we've eaten dinner, played five hands of poker and my sides hurt from laughing so hard. My mom has told Milo every embarrassing story she can think of from my childhood, my father is treating him like the son he never had, and I'm about to lose it.

Cock-blocked by my own parents.

"Thank you for the advice, Harvey. I've been meaning to stock my liquor cabinet, and I think some Bahamian rum would be a great addition." Milo rubs his hands together.

"I usually do mixed drinks for my New Year's Eve parties, and it'll be great to bring out some new recipes. You guys should come. It's a costume party. I bet you'd love it."

My dad points at him and then turns to me. "I like this one, buttercup."

Milo's eyes light up. "Why do you call her buttercup? Is there a story behind that?"

I roll my eyes. "The same story as every other girl at my school. We all loved that movie, *The Princess Bride.* I could recite all the lines."

"And she did," my mom interjects. "I was so tired of Buttercup and her nonsense. Who would leave a man like that?"

Ariana leans over, keeping her voice low so that no one will overhear. "You're trying to figure out how to get rid of them, aren't you?"

"Help me out, would ya? You're the one with all the ideas."

Ari shrugs. "I don't think you want my help. Because I'll tell them you're sexually frustrated after working overtime all week and need some bam-bam time with your boo."

"Oh my god."

My heated whisper draws Milo's attention. He raises his eyebrows, and I point to my watch.

"Trust me," Ari whispers. "Considering how much your mom wants grandkids, she'd probably be completely on board with that plan."

As gross as it is, she's not wrong.

My mom has always been an independent woman with her own career. Both of my parents were college professors, and they met at a conference. Over the years she emphasized the importance of not losing myself for a man.

But something strange happened a few years ago. She lost about fifty years off her feminism when her friends started having grandkids.

I have no doubt that my mom would make herself *extremely* scarce if she thought it meant there'd be a baby bouncing on her knee nine months from now.

But it turns out my dad is the one who saves the day.

"Well, Martine, I think we should leave these young people to it." He stands slowly, and I hop up to help him but then pause because Milo is already there.

My heart was already one big melted marshmallow after watching him be so attentive and sweet to my parents, but whatever resistance I had left is gone seeing Milo offer his arm to my father. He does it so easily, like it's second nature and not an imposition at all.

And in that moment, I'm forced to accept it. I've broken all the rules. Weirdness and professionalism be damned.

I'm in love with Milo.

If he doesn't feel the same way, the heartache I experienced after Will left is going to seem like child's play.

My mom pulls me into an embrace, and the hug seems a little tighter than usual. When I finally pull back, her eyes are bright.

"What is it, Mom? Is everything okay with you and Daddy?"

She regards me affectionately. "Just happy to see you smiling again, baby girl. We were worried about you for a long time." Her eyes slide over to Milo. "But you've found a man who doesn't need to dim your shine to make his own seem brighter. I can see I don't need to worry anymore. Not with the way that man looks at you. Mmm, hmm."

My face flames, but she just chuckles and kisses my cheek lightly. "I swear you kids forget that we were young and frisky once, too."

"I don't think I need to know too much about when you were frisky, Mom."

She just laughs as she hugs Ariana goodbye. After they've both hugged Milo, I walk them to the door and wait until they're in the elevator. When I get back inside the apartment, Ari is gone, and Milo is in the kitchen putting away the leftover food.

"You don't have to do that."

I feel bad enough that he's been stuck here for two hours entertaining my parents when I know he was looking forward to relaxing after a long week.

"No big deal. I'm almost done." Milo sticks a plastic container into the refrigerator and then drops the dishtowel in his hand on the counter.

"You were great with them. My dad is usually

surrounded by estrogen, so I think he really enjoyed having you here. Although I'm sorry I couldn't warn you. They sometimes just get the idea to pop by and start cooking. They're convinced that Ari and I will starve to death if they don't come check on us periodically."

Milo wraps an arm around my waist. "You don't need to apologize for having parents who care. I thought they were great. It's obvious how much they love you. It's not like I don't understand how they feel."

We're dancing around saying the words. It's right there on the tip of my tongue, and my pulse speeds up as I prepare to lay it all on the line.

But what comes out is, "Will you stay with me tonight?"

Coward, my inner voice taunts.

It's not quite what I wanted to say, but maybe it's a way to ease into it. Even with as much time as we've spent together over the past two weeks, we still haven't spent a whole night together. It's like this unspoken line that we haven't crossed.

But if Milo stays all night, then I can build up to telling him what these past few weeks have meant to me. So much has happened so fast, but I want him to know how I'm feeling.

Then it all comes crashing down.

"You know, I never thought I'd say this, but I honestly

don't feel like fucking." Milo hangs his head in mock shame. "This is rock bottom."

I laugh weakly. "We can just relax and watch some TV then. We've both been hunching over our computers a lot, but I give really good back massages."

Warnings are blaring in the back of my mind.

Danger.

Desperation alert.

It's like I can hear myself and I'm trying to stop the words falling out of my mouth, but I can't. I just keep digging the hole deeper.

"I even bought almond milk and those little cream cookies you like. The weather is supposed to be nice this weekend, so it should be perfect for us to get out and get some fresh air."

With every word out of my mouth, Milo retreats further and further. Physically he's still there, but I can feel him pulling inward. Until finally, he kisses my forehead.

"Are you trying to take care of me, Mya?"

There's a hint of amusement in his voice. Almost like he's laughing at me.

That hurts more than the rejection.

"I have a lot of errands to run, actually, so I'd better go. I'll see you on Monday."

I watch helplessly as he puts on his coat and the door shuts behind him.

ARIANA MUST HAVE radar because she gives me plenty of space after he leaves. I go through the motions of tidying the living room before retreating to my room and changing into my oldest, comfiest pajamas.

Why did I ask him to stay?

As I'm brushing my teeth, I mentally review all the reasons getting in deep with Milo is a bad idea. I've always been a list maker, so it's only natural. Maybe a list of all the reasons this is a terrible idea will convince my head, heart, and that brazen hussy between my thighs to stick with the program.

- *Pro: Makes me feel alive.*
- *Con: Emotionally unavailable.*

My heart sinks a little at that one. Milo has never brought a girlfriend to any company event or even referred to any of the women in his life in a permanent way. Why would I think I'd be the exception?

- *Pro: Takes great care of me when I'm drunk and ridiculous.*
- *Con: Um...*

Ok, there's really no downside to that one. The memory of Milo cooking me breakfast in his underwear will forever be #boyfriendgoals. He's the best boyfriend I've ever had except for the *teensy, eensy,* little part about him not actually being mine.

- *Pro: Smart and supports my career!*
- *Con: He's your biggest competition.*

A smile crosses my lips. Being my competition isn't as much of a negative as I originally thought it would be. Competing with Milo is strangely a turn on. Mainly because I love watching his brain at work. He seems to enjoy that with me as well, which has been a lovely surprise.

- *Pro: He's a god in bed.*
- *Con: Goes through women like tissues.*

I spit out the toothpaste. That right there is reason enough for me to back off. He likes being footloose and screwing different women in bar bathrooms on the weekends. He likes his life the way it is. Why would he want to change it?

- *Pro: I love him.*
- *Con: Doesn't love me back.*

List making isn't really as effective as it used to be. It's honestly just making me feel stupid that I thought he was feeling the same thing. Did I really think that a few weeks with me would turn him into boyfriend material?

A light knock at the door startles me. I wipe my face on the towel. It's probably one of our neighbors asking for a favor or something. But when I look through the peephole, it's Milo's face I see staring back.

There's a part of me that wants to be childish and leave him out there, but I open the door with a smile on my face so wide it makes my cheeks hurt. I'm not letting him know how much he hurt me.

"Hey, I thought you went home?"

There, that sounds appropriately unbothered, right?

Milo yanks me into his arms and his mouth covers mine. The anger I'm carrying translates directly into the kiss and I bite and lick at him, furious and turned on at the same time.

A door slams and we reluctantly pull apart. My neighbor a few doors down pushes her walker slowly down the hallway.

Squeak.

Squeak.

Squeak.

"Evening, Mya."

"Evening, Mrs. Abernathy."

Milo opens his mouth to speak but stops as the sound of the wheels get closer and closer.

Squeak.

Squeak.

Squeak.

Despite my determination to be mad, it's hilarious watching him trying to rein in whatever he was about to say. I know it's hard, but I only hope he can hold it. Our conversations tend to not be elderly-neighbor appropriate.

Once the elevator doors close behind Mrs. Abernathy, Milo pulls me back into his arms. "I fucked up. I'm sorry."

"You don't have to apologize for not wanting to stay over."

"That's not what I'm doing. I'm apologizing for being a chicken shit. I've had a bad experience before, but that's no excuse for walking out like that. You're nothing like Tessa. I've been driving around in a circle for the past half hour because despite what I said, I don't want to go home without you."

Emotion wells, but I tamp it back down just as quickly.

"Maybe you were right. Sleeping over has never been our thing. We're just having fun and keeping it casual. That's what we agreed to, right?"

"Fuck what we agreed to." His forehead falls to mine. "I'm going to fuck up sometimes, but you've gotta give me a chance to get it right. Come home with me. Please."

My fingers curl into his shirt. "I'm already in my pajamas."

His chest rocks with his laughter. "My car won't judge your attire, I promise."

"I'm not sure."

Of course, I really want to jump in his arms and never leave but I also don't want to spend the night if he's only doing it for me. If we're going to take this step, it needs to be what we both want. Never again do I want to be in a relationship where I'm the only one invested.

He sighs heavily. "I guess we could stay here. Although considering the pervy things I want to do to you, I'm not sure you want your roommate listening in."

Suddenly Ari's voice yells from behind me. "Headphones on. Can't hear a thing!"

We both dissolve into laughter.

"Also, I really want you to come. I want to go to sleep with you. And wake up with you. You're not the only one who wants to take things to the next level here. I'm sorry that I made you feel that way."

"You caught that, huh?"

It's alarming how easily he sees through my cool facade. He reads me like a book sometimes, and I'm not entirely sure how I feel about that. A girl needs a few secrets.

"I wouldn't be much of a boyfriend if I didn't catch that."

My eyes fly to his, searching the blue depths for meaning. He called himself my boyfriend earlier to my mom, but I figured that was due to lack of a better term. *Coworker I'm having casual sex with and also pretending to be engaged to*, just doesn't flow easily off the tongue.

"Well, you entertained my parents and cleaned up the kitchen without being asked. Then you apologized. I'd say as far as boyfriends go, you're doing okay so far."

His hands slide lower under my ass as he hoists me into his arms. "Good. I aim to please. Now, let's get your stuff. Because as cute as those pajamas are, you can't wear those all weekend."

All weekend?

Definitely #boyfriendgoals.

nineteen

MILO

I WAKE up the next morning freezing below the waist. The covers are scrunched up in the middle of the bed and my naked ass is in the wind.

But Mya is in my bed.

She's on her stomach, one leg kicked up as she clutches the stolen sheets to her chest. Her hair has come loose from her braid and sticks to her forehead. She's smiling in her sleep.

Waking up with Mya is quickly becoming my new favorite thing.

The clock on my nightstand tells me it's noon, but I'm having trouble believing it. With my insomnia, it's extremely rare for me to sleep past six in the morning, and that's only if I'm exhausted. But then I remember all the ways Mya exhausted me last night. I lay back against the pillows with a sated sigh, enjoying the chance to be a little lazy.

I have a to-do list a mile long and couldn't care less what is going undone. I finally have the woman of my dreams right where I want her.

In my bed.

"Why are you over there talking to yourself when it's so early?" Mya mumbles, pulling the sheet over her head.

"Was I? Sorry, I didn't realize. But I have to inform you that it's actually almost lunchtime."

She grumbles and it's so adorable that I don't even care she just snatched the last bit of linen covering me. Butterball ass naked is fine with me.

"If I haven't had coffee yet, then it's early."

"Duly noted." I climb out of bed and walk into my closet to find a pair of sweatpants.

Mya is snoring when I come out. She's still snoring when I return ten minutes later with a cup of coffee and a tray with toast and scrambled eggs.

Her head pops up when I sit on the edge of the bed. "Is that coffee? Oh my god, you're the best."

Another thing to add to the Mya files, coffee is a must. Once she's had a few sips, the line in the middle of her forehead relaxes and she looks less like she might stab me.

"Welcome back to the land of the living. You went a little *Walking Dead* on me for a minute there."

She laughs and shoves my shoulder. "Shut up. Not all of us can look like we just fell off a billboard first thing in the morning."

"You look gorgeous all the time. And you'll look even better when you're naked in the shower with me."

Mya is grinning like a loon as I take her coffee mug and set it on the night table. I grab her hands and tug her from the bed.

"Come on, troublemaker. I've been fantasizing about getting you in this shower ever since I got it redone."

"Have you?" Mya hops into my arms and wraps her legs around me. I carry her into the bathroom and set her down gently.

"I am willing to admit that I've pictured you in my shower a time or two. Or fifty." I move behind her and sweep her hair over her shoulder, baring the fragrant skin to my touch. I kiss the hollow of her throat then her collarbone, my lips leaving a moist trail.

"Tell me what you imagined," she breathes. She sends me a cheeky look over her shoulder before pressing her round bottom against me. She smiles when my fingers tighten around her arm.

"You, naked and wet. All these amazing curves covered in suds." I skim my hands up her belly and cup her breasts, the tight peaks of her nipples pressing into the center of my palms. She melts against me as she surrenders to the sensations my fluttering fingers create.

She turns in my arms and pulls me down for her kiss. I kiss her mouth as if making love to it, intense in my exploration, my tongue thrusting against hers intimately. I grind against her, nestling my cock directly over her clit.

The feeling of bare skin reminds me that I need to grab protection.

If I let things progress too far, I won't have the willpower to stop myself from taking her skin-to-skin. I give her a quick kiss and jog back into the bedroom to get the box of condoms. By the time I return, I already have a condom in place. I set the box carefully on the edge of the counter closest to the shower.

"Get up on the counter."

My voice is rough with lust, and I can see the answering desire in her eyes. My command excites her. She hops up on the counter and crosses her legs in a sultry pose.

"Open your legs. Show me that pretty pussy."

Mya flushes, but after a beat, she obeys. Swallowing against the surge of animal lust I feel looking down at her bare, pink pussy, I shake my head to clear it. With Mya, I want more than just the physical pleasure of release.

I want to give her a level of satisfaction no man has ever given her, make her crazy. I want to leave my mark on her.

"Damn you're beautiful."

I stroke the sensitive skin of her thighs. She shudders and tries to close her legs instinctively as I continue to tease her. Her eyes drift closed, and she whimpers softly.

"I love how you touch me..." Her brown eyes are dewy when she reopens them, and she twines her arms around my neck.

My hand stays where it is, playing gently in her wetness, toying with her clit until she squirms. I wait until her eyes are frantic with wanting, until she has to acknowledge who holds her pleasure. She looks up at me, her eyes begging.

Then I enter her with a thick thrust that steals both of our breath. I pound her hard and fast, unable to hold back the urgency I feel.

I've had her slow and sweet, and now I need her all at once.

I want to consume her with big, greedy bites.

She obviously feels the same rush because she urges me on with her nails in my forearms and her heels at my ass. I know she's getting close to another orgasm when she coils her legs around me, tightening like a vise.

"Milo, please!" She grips my forearms and wails, her nails leaving tiny crescent indentations in my skin.

I'm too close to completion to slow my pace, too far gone to gentle the force of my thrusts even as her pussy tightens around me. She shudders violently, absorbing the force of my pounding. I hold her under the arms, clasping her to me as my own release takes over. All my joints and every muscle lock up in intense pleasure as my orgasm rips through me.

When it's over, we both lay against the counter, panting and spent. I look up and meet my eyes in the mirror behind Mya's head. I look as if I've just run a marathon.

"Damn, girl. You're a workout."

I pull out gently, part of me reluctant to leave her warmth. I help her up from her awkward position cramped over the counter.

Mya snorts out a laugh and runs a gentle hand through my damp hair. "I think we can both use that shower now."

I reach in and turn on the dual showerheads, adjusting the temperature until it's perfect. She coils her long hair up into a knot on top of her head before she follows me under the streaming water.

"This is absolute heaven." She sighs as the water hits her back, rolling her shoulders to relieve the tension. "I've only seen these in magazines."

"I went a little overboard in here, I guess. I couldn't afford stuff like this growing up so it's hard not to buy it now that it's within reach."

She opens her eyes, and her gaze is like getting hit with high beams. Last night we stayed up late talking about our lives growing up and somehow segued into talking about our past relationships. After my comment about Tessa, she was curious. I told her the whole story, and surprisingly, it wasn't as difficult to talk about this time.

There's something about Mya that makes it easy to talk about anything.

"You've worked hard for everything you've achieved. You deserve good things." She taps my chest lightly to emphasize her words.

"Does that include you?" I clear my throat and pick up a bar of soap as an excuse to look away.

When I turn back to her, she stands up on her toes and kisses me square on the mouth. "You think I'm a good thing?"

"I think you're the best thing." I hold her gaze as I say it, knowing that I've never spoken truer words.

Our connection is deeply sexual of course, a dead man would want her, but more than that I want her to trust me to take care of her. I want her to turn to me for all her needs, physical and emotional. I want no more secrets between us.

"I've never felt like this about anyone, Mya. But damn if I know what to do about it."

Talking about feelings isn't easy for me, but I need her to know this isn't a casual thing for me anymore. Due to my checkered past, I'm worried that she'll continue to think that this whole thing is just about sex.

It might have started as scratching a sexual itch, but

every moment we've spent together has led to this, my overwhelming need to have her in my life.

She shakes her head and laughs shyly, covering her mouth with her hand. "You are such a puzzle, Hamilton, because after yesterday, I was sure that you didn't feel the same way."

"I'm sorry about yesterday."

Her hands find their way to my cheeks, and she holds my face between her palms gently. The way she's looking at me... a man could live on that look alone.

"Yesterday is over. I'm living in the now. And what I'm feeling right now is something I've never felt before either."

———

THE NEXT DAY finds me relaxing on the couch while Mya enjoys a shower alone. I've been banished since, according to Mya, she never really gets to shower properly when I'm in there.

Something about my dick taking up too much room.

Well, that's not what she said but that's what I heard. I'm taking it as a compliment. Or that she's sore from too much sex.

My cell phone rings, and I snatch it up when I see my mom's name.

"Hello, son. Is this a bad time?"

"No, I'm just relaxing at home."

You can almost hear the shock through the phone. Then she says, "Hold on. Ten, your brother's on the phone! And he's not working for once."

I laugh at that. "Funny. What are you two up to this morning?"

"Church. I figured your brother could use a little prayer. Please tell me you're really relaxing in that beautiful apartment you pay so much for and this isn't a joke."

"Mom, I'm actually at home. Things are going well at work. I won't have to work such long hours forever. But I'm glad you called." I pause, surprisingly shy about what I'm about to ask. "I wanted to ask if you still have Grandma's ring."

It's so quiet I pull back to look at my phone to make sure we haven't lost the connection.

"Mom, you still there?"

"Yes. I was just so surprised. Milo, you haven't even mentioned seeing anyone."

I fiddle with a loose thread on my shorts. "Actually, do you remember my coworker, Mya? You met her when you came up for the company holiday party last year."

She gasps. "I knew it! I told Ten you had a crush on that girl. Didn't I say that, Ten?"

I can hear my brother's irritated grumble in the

background. Then I hear the sound of the bathroom door opening. Mya must be done with her shower.

"I'm not saying I'm proposing or anything. Things are still new. I was just wondering... She's different than anyone I've ever been with before, and I would really like you and Ten to come visit so you can meet her properly."

"I would love that, honey. Grandma's ring is in the bottom of my jewelry box. I've been hanging on to it for the day one of you boys met your match."

Mya sits on the couch next to me. Her hair is pulled back into a high bun, and she still has droplets of water on her neck. With no makeup and wearing one of my old T-shirts, she's the most beautiful thing I've ever seen. My grandmother's ring would look perfect on her finger, actually. It's exactly her style.

The thought would have had me running away just a month ago, but now it makes me smile.

"She's more than a match for me, Mom, and I can't wait for you to meet her."

Mya looks over at me in surprise when she finally figures out who I'm talking to. Her cheeks go pink with pleasure, which makes me want to lean over and take a bite out of her.

"Okay, Mom. Enjoy church. Bye."

After I hang up, Mya grabs the phone and then climbs in my lap. "You told your mother about me?"

The smile on my face feels so natural. How long has it been since I've been this unbelievably happy? Never. That sounds about right.

"I did. She remembers meeting you at the party, but I told her I want her and Ten to come visit so you can spend some time together."

She suddenly won't meet my eyes. "This is all happening so fast. I'm scared to be this happy."

Before she can say anything else, my phone dings with an alert. A few seconds later, Mya's phone chimes. Frowning, she picks it up from the couch.

"It's an email from James. Mr. Lavin is going to be in town tomorrow. James scheduled a meeting." She bites her lip.

"This is what we knew would happen. We're ready. We've been ready. Now it's time to lock it down. Nothing is going to stop us from getting this account."

"I just thought we'd have more time." She won't meet my eyes. "Once Mr. Lavin picks a campaign, things will be different."

"You mean we'll go back to being mortal enemies then?" She doesn't laugh.

I tip up her chin, forcing her to look at me. The worry in her brown eyes tugs at my heartstrings. "Mya, no matter who wins the account, that has nothing to do with what's going on between us. It won't change anything."

"Promise? You hate to lose."

Her voice is small, something I'm not used to from her.

That's what lets me know that this is a very real fear for her. And I don't want her worrying about this for even one minute.

"I promise. And yes, I hate to lose. But I would hate to lose what we have here more."

Mya nods slowly.

That's when her words hit me. "Wait, did you just say I hate to lose as if you're sure you're going to win tomorrow? Brat." I tickle her, and she dissolves into giggles.

I like that sound much better.

twenty

MYA

WE'VE PRACTICED AND PREPARED. Our presentations are as technically perfect as they're going to get, but that means nothing if we can't get them to play.

"Hell of a time for my laptop to crap out." Milo yanks at his hair. He looks like he's on the verge of rupturing a vein.

Last night, we loaded both presentations on his laptop since I'd forgotten to bring mine along. Plus, all of our files are saved on the company cloud drive, so neither of us thought it was a big deal. We even tested it again first thing this morning. Everything was fine.

But now his laptop has the blue screen of death, and Mr. Lavin and the rest of his team are due any moment. I can actually feel my blood pressure climbing higher and higher.

"Do you need your stress cow?" Milo teases.

"No." *Yes.* But there's no way I'm squeezing that thing anywhere a client might see.

"Don't worry honey. My dick doesn't mind if you use him as a squeeze toy if you get nervous."

I hate that he can make me smile in the middle of a crisis. Because I don't want to laugh right now. Things are falling apart!

As usual, Milo can sense when I'm about to go off the rails.

He rubs my arms briskly. "Let's not panic. It's not like our work is lost. Just go borrow Wallace's laptop and run the presentation from his. I'm sure he won't mind."

My steps are careful and measured as I walk out of the conference room, but I spring into a run as soon as I clear the door. I'm trying to remain calm so I don't freak Milo out, but I'm seriously hoping these technical difficulties aren't some kind of omen.

Wallace looks up when I reach his cubicle.

"So sorry to do this to you, but I need your laptop. Milo's is dead, and I forgot mine at home. The Lavin team will be here any minute."

He immediately starts closing the windows he's working in. "Sure thing. I'll switch and use the desktop in that empty cubicle across from Kevin's office."

My shoulders sag with relief. "Thank you. I have just

enough time to log in to the company server and download the presentation before they get here."

After Wallace logs out, I log on to the company intranet with my own username and password and start downloading the presentation. It's graphics heavy and will probably take a few minutes, so I carry the laptop in my arms as I walk back to the conference room.

The door is still ajar from when I left. The sound of angry but hushed voices reaches me before I get there.

"I told you in Vegas, I'm handling everything. There's no need for you to talk to Mya."

My mouth drops open. I recognize Milo's voice, but then my surprise turns to fury when I realize who he's talking to.

Andre Lavin.

I should storm the room and demand to know what is going on. But instead I look around frantically and then dive into the first open door nearby, which turns out to be a janitor's closet. The sharp tang of chemicals assaults my nose, but I hold very still as footsteps rush past. I edge the door open and watch Mr. Lavin's back as he strides down the hallway to the reception area.

Is he leaving?

Probably. Why stay for the presentations when he obviously has some sort of backend deal arranged with Milo already?

My heart is beating so hard that I press a shaky hand to my chest as if that'll stop it from breaking in half. Everything that's happened over the past few weeks suddenly seems different in light of what I just heard.

Milo's utter confidence that we had this thing in the bag, his insistence that we work on our campaigns together.

It's all been part of his plan to make sure that *he's* the one leading this account.

If he's been communicating with Mr. Lavin directly, then he has all the info needed to be sure his campaign is exactly what the client wants.

And I'm the trusting, naive idiot who fell for it.

The laptop chimes and I look down to see that our presentations are done downloading. All this work was for nothing. That's when I decide I'm done hiding.

I burst from the closet and march across the hall and into the conference room. Milo looks up in surprise from where he's tapping away at his laptop keyboard.

"It's still dead. Oh good, you got Wallace's instead. Any trouble downloading the presentations?"

He's talking to me as if nothing is wrong. As if nothing has changed. But for me, it's like everything has been scorched to ash.

"I did, not that it matters. I heard you talking to Mr. Lavin, so I'm not sure why we should even go through with this presentation when you've already told him you're leading this account."

Milo freezes bent over the laptop. Only his eyes move to meet mine. "What did you hear?"

"Enough to know you're a liar and you've been playing me this whole time. I can't believe I trusted you. *'We'll compete for this account fair and square, Mya.'* I'm an idiot. But not anymore. Does James know about this?"

"James has nothing to do with this."

I cut him off. "Good because we're going to present, and then we're going to let him decide. I'm not sure what you promised Mr. Lavin in exchange for choosing your campaign, but it doesn't matter now. As soon as this presentation is over, we'll see what James has to say."

He looks behind me frantically. "It's not what you think. You have to let me explain."

"There's no time for that. Besides, your words are just as fake as our relationship."

A sound at the door causes us both to pause. I turn to see Andre Lavin standing in the doorway watching us.

Shit.

"Mr. Lavin, I'm sorry–"

James rushes into the room then, and the rest of the Lavin team follows him. My eyes stay on Mr. Lavin's until there's too much activity in the room to maintain eye contact. I'm not even sure what I was trying to say before.

I'm sorry we lied.

Please don't tell our boss.

This entire web of lies is unraveling so fast that I'm tripping over them.

"Excellent, we're all here. Thank you for granting us your time today, Mr. Lavin. I know that you and your team are extremely busy. But we have two fantastic campaigns prepared for you to evaluate." James turns to me and then looks at Milo. "Are we ready?"

I look over at Mr. Lavin. His dark eyes reveal nothing. But he doesn't appear inclined to tell James what he overheard either, so I guess that means the show must go on.

We'll have to do the presentations even though there's absolutely no chance we're getting the job.

And I'll have to stand next to Milo even though my heart is breaking.

———

AS SOON AS the lights come back on, I walk over to the Lavin team and shake each of their hands. But the effect is probably ruined because I can't look anyone in the eye. Andre Lavin shakes hands with James before leaving the room.

James seems startled by the abrupt departure. "Well,

that was odd. Great job, guys." Then he gathers his things and leaves.

I don't look at Milo as I do the same.

"Mya, please wait." He grabs my arm as I walk by.

I shake off his grip and keep walking. Then I go to the one place he can't follow me, the women's restroom. I barricade myself in a stall and spend the next ten minutes fighting tears. No one is going to see me cry over this.

My professional reputation is that of a woman who is calm, confident and in control. Even if I'm not exactly sure how I'll explain this all to James yet, I know that the image I want to present is the same one I've spent the last five years building.

Someone who is in control and not *being* controlled.

"Mya? Are you in there?" Anya's voice comes from the next stall.

"Yes. I'm here."

"Not to be nosy or anything, but Milo asked me to check on you. Are you okay?"

That makes me want to cry again. Because now I know that all the little things he's been doing aren't just sweet, thoughtful things. It's him keeping tabs on his competitor.

How he must have laughed behind my back when he went home!

"Not really, but I don't want him to know that."

Anya is quiet for a moment. "Men suck."

Her words manage to get a laugh out of me when I wouldn't have thought it was possible, so I guess that's something.

"Yeah. Look, can you do me a favor and get my handbag from my office? I need to get out of here, and I really don't want to see him."

I hear the sound of the stall door being unlocked. "Of course. In fact, on the way back I'll remind James that he meant to ask Milo about the Adler account. That way, he'll be busy and you can sneak out."

"You're saving my life right now."

"We girls have to stick together. Believe me I've been there."

Five minutes later, the bathroom door opens. I unlock my stall and peer out.

Anya hands me my bag with a smile. "They're in James's office now. Go. I'll tell James that you had female problems. He'll be too traumatized to ask any questions. Trust me. It works every time."

I thank her again and then rush out. Fate does me a solid, because when I check Uber, there's a car right around the corner. By the time I get downstairs, the car is pulling up.

Right now I just need to be alone so I can think.

And grieve.

The last few weeks have felt like an awakening of sorts.

It was about so much more than just the job. I felt like I found a comfort zone between Mya, the professional and Mya, the woman. Moving on from the baggage of my last relationship, I learned a lot about what I want in a man and who I want to be, but now I'm left to wonder what it all means.

I'm in love with him, but for him, this has all been a game.

Damn. Maybe I haven't learned as much as I thought.

There are no lights in the windows of the apartment when we pull up. I can't remember if Ariana was on shift today, but I can only hope she's not home. This is definitely a situation that calls for a bit of a pity cry. Alone.

I say goodbye to the Uber driver, promising to give her five stars. I'm turning my key in the front door when a shadow moves to my right.

"What the hell?" I shriek and drop my keys in surprise.

"Whoa! It's me! Mya, baby, it's me."

Even though my heart is still in my throat, I calm slightly when I recognize Will's voice.

"Will? What are you doing in my hallway?"

"Just wanted to check on you. After those texts you sent last night I had to see you." He smiles, and I'm reminded of how cute he is.

He's still wearing his suit, so I know he came straight from work. He's always reminded me of the actor Will

Smith, tall, lanky and a little goofy. We used to joke that they were long-lost brothers since they shared similar looks and the same nickname.

Then his words register.

Last night?

At the look on my face his grin falters. "You don't remember texting me last night?"

Eyeing him warily, I pull my phone out of my bag and hit the icon for texts. Before going to bed, I'd texted Ariana a playful "Missing you!" along with a kissy face emoji.

Turns out, I was messaging Will.

"That was meant for Ariana, actually."

His face falls. "When I saw that, I figured it meant you were thinking about me too. You know, since yesterday..."

It dawns on me that yesterday would have been our wedding date. No wonder Will thought the message was meant for him. If things had gone according to plan, we would be on our honeymoon right now.

"I didn't even realize the date. Sorry about that." I'm just glad it wasn't something worse. Some of the messages Ari and I send back and forth don't ever need to see the light of day. "At least I wasn't drunk dialing like Ari was when we got margaritas a few weeks ago."

"Margaritas?" Now he sounds intrigued. "You've never been much of a drinker."

"Well, things change. We went out drinking at this new

tapas bar, and it was a blast. Apparently, I danced on the bar."

He shakes his head slightly. "I can't even imagine that. But I guess that means you had fun. That's good. You sound happy."

For the first time since we broke up, I'm not reading subtext into what he's saying or assuming that he has an ulterior motive. I'm just taking his words at face value.

Because you don't care what he thinks, I realize.

It's a liberating thought after so many years using his words and opinions as the litmus for how I lived my life.

Now whether he approves or not has no effect on me. I'm secure in the knowledge that the people who really care about me aren't judging me or waiting for me to make mistakes so they can rub my face in it.

With a little distance, I can also admit that maybe Will wasn't trying to do that either. He has his share of flaws just like anyone else, but he's not the monster I'd built him up to be after the breakup.

Maybe it's possible that Will and I are both good people, just not good for each other. And that's completely okay.

"I am happy," I finally respond.

And it's true.

Despite what happened today, I feel pretty damn good about how my life is going right now. Things might be over with Milo but I'm not going to let that take away from everything else I've achieved. I have a great family, a best friend and roomie who would do anything for me, and I have ice cream in my freezer.

Hey, I'm trying to look at the bright side here.

Will rubs the back of his neck. "When I saw your text, I thought it meant that you were ready to talk. You never responded to the flowers or returned any of my calls before so..."

Now I kind of feel like a bitch. "I wasn't ready to talk then."

"I deserve that after the way I ended things. I'm sorry, Mya. I think I just got scared. Marriage seems like such a big step."

"It is a big step. Maybe it's better that you called it off when you did."

His eyes meet mine, searching. "But that's just it. Things aren't better. I miss you. I miss talking to you. I'd love to take you out to dinner sometime. Or drinks, if that's your thing now."

My heart thumps and then starts racing. Just a few months ago, hearing that Will missed me would have been the highlight of my day. All I'd wanted was for him to say that leaving was a mistake and that all our years together meant more to him than just settling for what was comfortable. But now that the moment is here, I can't dredge up anything other than emptiness.

"Will, I'm glad that you apologized. What you did hurt me, and I think clearing the air is a good thing. I don't want to look back on our time together with regret."

"I don't either! I just want things to go back to the way they used to be." Will takes my hand and squeezes it.

That used to be our thing, our secret signal to say we loved each other even when we were in a crowded room.

But now that gesture feels empty. Hollow, just like this conversation. It feels disloyal to be squeezing hands with him when I know that my heart isn't in it.

"Things have been over between us for six months. That's a long time. I've moved on. You should too."

He looks like he wants to argue, but then he slowly lets go of my hand. "I guess I figured things out too late, huh?"

"Yeah, you did."

I can't deny it feels good to get that little dig in. I'm only human, so let me have that one.

"We weren't meant to be, Will. I deserve someone who wants the woman I am, not who he thinks I should be. And so do you. Go out there and find that for yourself. Everyone deserves that."

We were together for a long time, so it feels strange to know this is likely the last time we'll ever see each other. I stand on tiptoe and kiss his cheek.

Then I go in my apartment to find my ice cream and figure out how to take my own advice.

twenty-one
MILO

REGRET IS A POWERFUL DRUG.

Over the past two days, I've played out every possible scenario that could have occurred after Mya overheard me talking to Mr. Lavin.

I should have picked her up, thrown her over my shoulder, and forced her to hear me out.

I should have told Andre Lavin to back off my girl instead of being diplomatic about it.

I should have told James that the client was expressing personal interest in Mya and let him handle it.

Should have done doesn't change what happened though. All the *should haves* in the world won't make her talk to me.

I've called her so many times that I'm pretty sure a restraining order is forthcoming.

When I stopped by her place, I could hear the TV on in the background, but no one would answer. I knocked on the door until an older woman stuck her head out into the hallway and gave me the evil eye.

Sometimes you have to know when to admit defeat.

Now I'm here at work getting absolutely nothing done while my co-workers tiptoe around me. Yeah, I'm in a shitty mood. And I'm not even bothering to hide it.

We're not going to get the account, and I'll be lucky to still have a job once James finds out why.

My phone rings, and I wince when I see James's name pop up. I've been avoiding him all day. Guilt will do that to you.

But if this is it, then I might as well face the music with dignity.

"Hey, James."

"If you've got a second, can you stop by my office?"

"Sure. I'll come now."

Walking down the hallway, I start noticing things I've never paid attention to before. The paint is fading slightly. I remember when the color was changed from white to something called ecru, whatever the fuck that is. The carpet is still the same though.

Funny the things you notice when you're on your way to be fired. I have the urge to yell out *dead man walking* at everyone I pass.

When I get to James's office, he motions for me to close the door.

"I'm not sure how to say this," he begins.

"You don't have to be delicate. Just lay it on me." If I'm about to be sacked, I'd rather hear it upfront than after an hour of bullshit.

"Fine. Andre Lavin called me asking for Mya's phone number. I gave it to him, but I didn't feel right about not saying something. I get the sense that he wasn't interested in calling her about the campaign."

My relief that I'm not fired immediately morphs into sick jealousy. The very thing I was trying to prevent when I started this whole thing in Vegas has happened anyway.

"He was interested from the moment he met her. I guess it was inevitable that he'd only wait so long."

James looks disturbed. "I have to say, I'm surprised that you're taking this so well. And I'm very surprised that Mr. Lavin would pursue her despite knowing that she's already engaged."

I can't very well explain that Mr. Lavin is going after Mya because he knows our engagement is fake. If he hasn't blown the whistle on us yet, then maybe he doesn't plan to.

He probably doesn't feel the need to. After tonight, he'll have what he wants; Mya designing his campaign and warming his bed.

My hands clench into fists.

"Did he say anything else?"

James shakes his head. "Not to me. But Anya said he asked about good local restaurants before she transferred his call."

After a minute passes with me still sitting there immobile, James throws his hands up in the air in frustration. "Why the hell are you still sitting here?"

It's too hard to explain when I can't tell him the whole truth, so I settle for the most important part. "Maybe this is what Mya wants. A rich, handsome guy. Isn't that what all women dream of?"

"I'm pretty sure Mya wants the man who actually cares about her. The one who'll be there in good times and in bad."

"It's too late. She won't talk to me. I lied to her about something important, and let's face it, I didn't exactly have a good track record to start with."

James fixes me with a glare. "I may have failed at marriage, but at least it taught me a little something about what not to do. Communication is key. Everything you just said to me, you need to say to her. Go fight for your girl! Maybe if I'd done that, my marriage wouldn't have fallen apart."

As he speaks, an energy grows until I'm too restless to sit. Mya changed something in me over the past few weeks.

She brought out the best in me while teaching me that it's okay to not be perfect.

Maybe a rich guy is what she wants, but maybe it isn't.

If there's even a chance she wants me, I need to know.

I turn back to James. "What was the name of the restaurant Anya recommended?"

MYA

IT TURNS out the *time-of-the-month* card is good for multiple days off from work. When I called in to check with James, he couldn't get off the phone fast enough.

Anya is a genius.

And I'm a wreck.

Taking my own advice is much easier said than done. Demanding the best is hard when your heart wants the thing you know is bad for it. My head is determined to hold on to my principles but my heart aches to answer the phone every time I see Milo's picture flash on the screen.

Which it's doing right now. He really is unfairly handsome.

I push the phone away with a scowl. I don't have time for handsome men and their excuses. I'm busy. There are

Netflix shows I need to watch. Just me and my stress cow against the world. My fingers give Chelsea a comforting squeeze.

Hey, don't judge. It really does make me feel better.

Ariana clears her throat.

Oh yeah, she's here too.

"I'm going to say something that you aren't going to like, but just hear me out." Her voice is muffled as she takes another spoonful of ice cream.

She resisted binge eating with me on day one, but even she has only so much willpower.

The power of Chunky Monkey is incontrovertible.

"Just say it. I don't really think anything you say could make this worse."

When Ari has something she wants to say, there's no holding her back anyway, whether you grant her permission or not. Plus, I kind of do want an outside perspective on this.

"William was a twat."

My mouth falls open. "Wait, what? I thought you liked him?"

She shrugs. "I didn't dislike him. Or at least I didn't until I noticed how he always put you down and never seemed to care about what you want. Everything was about him."

"What does it matter now? We've broken up."

I hate that I'm feeling defensive about this, but

somehow it feels like an attack, as if not seeing William's true colors is a reflection on my bad judgment.

"Which... maybe it is.

"Because I saw those roses you brought home a few weeks ago. Then you mentioned he came by yesterday. If there's even a chance that you two might get back together, I want it on record that I think you can do way better. You deserve someone who knows how awesome you are, Mya. And you didn't get excited when you talked about him. But do you know who you *did* get excited about?"

I hold up my hand. "Don't even say it. I don't want that name in my mental space. This is supposed to be an asshole-free zone!"

My hand clenches around Chelsea a few times.

"Jesus, stop squeezing that damn cow! It's kind of turning me on, and even I'm not that fucked up."

She heaves a dramatic sigh.

"Look, I'm just saying you should talk to him. Give him a chance to explain. Because that kind of chemistry doesn't come along every day."

Having said her piece, she rises gracefully, scooping up Oreo as she goes. Then she pauses.

"Also, whenever you and Will would fool around in your room, I'd always hear your vibrator after he left. You didn't have that problem with Milo. Just saying."

"Ari!" I slide down in my chair and put a throw pillow over my face.

Her laughter follows her out of the room. "No shame, girl. I'm just saying you shouldn't have to put up with a dude's shit and still have to take care of yourself. What the hell is the point of that?"

After she's gone I take the pillow off of my head and let out a sigh.

What the hell is *the point?*

Maybe I should at least hear him out. I would like to think that I've matured enough to know that things are not always black and white. Sometimes two people can be in the exact same situation but see it differently.

It's possible Milo didn't think he was being underhanded by talking to the client directly or that he was planning to tell me about it.

Ugh. Now I'm just rationalizing and trying to find a reason to forgive him.

Good sex isn't a reason to overlook lies and treachery. But we do work together, and I can't stay home eating Ben & Jerry's forever, so I probably need to talk to him sooner rather than later. Better to have this confrontation outside of the office.

I pick up my phone and skim all the *I'm sorry* and *Let me explain* texts. Then I notice a call from an unfamiliar number. The same number left a voicemail.

Miss Taylor, this is Andre Lavin. I heard from Mr. Lawson that you've been under the weather, and I'm sorry to hear that. But if possible, I would like to take you to dinner before I leave town. I'll be dining at Les Printemps tonight at 8pm. Join me if you can.

My loud *whoop* brings Ari running. Her robe flaps open behind her as she bursts into the room, Oreo yipping at her heels.

"What's going on? What happened?"

I struggle to my feet, sluggish after two days on the couch feeling sorry for myself. But I'm going to have to rally because this is my chance to explain my side of the story to Mr. Lavin.

More than likely I'll have to swallow my pride and grovel to make up for the lies we told in Vegas. But now that he's seen my campaign, maybe he's more inclined to forgive if it means getting a kickass launch for his new line.

"Andre Lavin wants to meet me for dinner. This is my chance. I have to convince him that Mirage can handle this account, despite everything that's happened. Because if I don't at least try to salvage this, I'll never forgive myself."

Ari nods along. "You've got this. Put your big girl panties on and go get that account. Well honestly, any panties other than the ones you're wearing will do because you've been on this couch for like two days straight."

See what I mean?

She never holds back.

———

GROVELING IS SUPPOSED to be hard work, but Mr. Lavin has been incredibly understanding. In fact, almost *too* understanding. Every time I try to explain what happened in Vegas, he redirects the conversation.

"Mr. Lavin, I really do want to apologize for lying to you. That was–"

He holds up a hand, pausing me mid-speech. "Andre. Please call me Andre."

"Right. As I was saying, we really didn't intend to be dishonest."

Mr. Lavin leans forward, starting to say something, but has to lean back when the waiter arrives. After hearing an impressive array of specials, I point randomly to something on the menu. Mr. Lavin orders filet mignon and a bottle of wine with a name that I can't pronounce.

I look around the restaurant. *Les Printemps* is a well-established, *very fancy*, restaurant and often a meeting place between the movers and shakers of DC. Now I'm here, wearing my best little black dress and dining with a client.

This feels surreal.

"Thank you for the invitation. I appreciate the opportunity. We didn't really have time to talk at the office."

"Of course," he purrs. "I've been intrigued by you from the start. Am I wrong that you felt it, too?"

I pause. Maybe this is a language-barrier thing, but I'm starting to get a little uncomfortable.

"Oh no, I've definitely been intrigued by Lavin Couture from the start. The way you mix the masculine and the feminine is groundbreaking. Your designs have ushered in a new way of thinking about the female form."

"*Cara mia*, I am *always* thinking about the female form."

His slow smile is so intimate that I can almost hear the woman at the next table sigh. Jeez, this guy just drips Italian charisma. You can almost get high from the pheromones.

I don't even think he realizes the effect he has. Flirting is just second nature to him.

"Of course. But in regard to the campaign—"

My eyes land on a man sitting right behind Mr. Lavin. He was seated a few minutes ago, but he barely registered. I've been completely focused on explaining my bad behavior. But when he shifts his menu to the left, I can't deny that something about the shape of those shoulders is really familiar.

"More wine, Mya?"

I snap back to attention. "No, thank you. It's probably

better if I don't, otherwise, I might forget everything I wanted to discuss."

He winks. "There is no need to rush, *bella*. We have all night."

"All night? Why would we have all night?"

Oh god, did I zone out and miss something?

Focus, Mya.

He pauses, his fingers on the stem of his wineglass. "Well, I assumed after dinner perhaps we could go dancing. Whatever you wish."

Something about the way he's looking at me makes me pause. My eyes bounce over the table, the single candle in the middle, the lily he presented me with when I arrived. If I hadn't come charging in here so focused on professional redemption, I would have seen it before.

This scenario looks nothing like a business meeting. The stage has been set for romance not business.

I'm on a date with Andre Lavin.

"Oh boy," I whisper under my breath.

If you'd asked me earlier if there was any way I could screw up this business arrangement any worse, I'd have assured you that we were already at rock bottom.

But now I'm on a date, *that I didn't know was a date*, talking about business while Mr. Lavin has apparently been talking about something else entirely.

As Ariana would say, *fuck a duck.*

"Mr. Lavin–"

"Andre," he corrects automatically.

"Right. This is awkward. I'm not really sure what to say. I wasn't aware this was a personal..." I struggle to find the right words, "meeting."

He leans across the table, his dark eyes never leaving mine. "You are a very beautiful woman, Mya. I find you intoxicating."

Despite not being interested at all, I find myself melting a little under that gaze.

Hey, don't judge me until you've sat in a dimly lit room across from a handsome billionaire while he calls you intoxicating.

Most women would have already thrown their panties at him.

"Wow. I honestly don't know what to say. This is a bit of a shock." And also, a potential landmine.

If I stay, I risk him getting the wrong idea.

If I go, then I might offend him and damage any chance there is of Mirage getting his business.

His eyes narrow slightly. "I was under the impression that you were aware of my interest ever since our first meeting in Las Vegas."

"When Milo told you he'd be the best fit for this job?

Yeah, I overheard you two talking. That's why I'm here. I wanted the chance to talk about my ideas for your campaign. I'm not sure what Milo told you, but I really feel that *my* ideas for marketing the groom's tuxedos alongside the bridal gowns will set you apart."

Andre sits back, his expression measured. "Is that what you think we talked about in Vegas? No, we didn't talk about the account. We talked about you."

"Me?"

"Mr. Hamilton was quite clear that he didn't appreciate my interest in you. He warned me to stay away from you."

"He did?"

My mind is racing, trying to fit this new knowledge in with my memories of the trip. How did Milo find time to speak to Mr. Lavin alone when we were together the whole time?

Mr. Lavin laughs softly. Even his laugh is elegant, a sort of low, rumbling growl. "It was very late after dinner when I encountered Mr. Hamilton at the bar. He made it clear that you were involved."

"We're not together. I mean, we're not a couple."

My heart clenches at the reminder. I've been so angry with Milo, thinking that he'd gone behind my back. More so, thinking that he'd valued business over our developing relationship.

But now I find out that he wasn't thinking about business at all, but rather that he was trying to protect me?

"Not many men would threaten the competition over a woman who's just a friend. You're lucky to have found someone who would do anything, even jeopardize his career, for you."

"Milo *threatened* you?"

My eyes seek out his. This close I can see the unusual shading of his striking dark eyes and smell the subtle aroma of his cologne. Any other woman would be drooling, but all I can think about are a pair of laughing blue eyes.

"You must have misunderstood."

"I assure you he was quite clear." Andre smiles wryly. "After our conversation, I was discouraged. I would not pursue a woman who is engaged to be married. But after what I overheard at your office..."

Just then a waiter comes to the table holding a plate aloft. When he lowers it, Milo's face appears. "Someone ordered a steak?"

"Milo?"

He drops the plate unceremoniously on the table and then slides into the booth next to me. Mr. Lavin watches, his eyes twinkling at the sudden turn of events. He doesn't even seem perturbed, just picks up the wine bottle again.

"Mr. Hamilton, I didn't know you'd be joining us. Wine?"

Milo glares at him before grabbing the bottle. "Don't mind if I do." He takes a swig directly from the bottle. "You didn't waste any time making your move, I see."

"I never waste time. Life is too short. We have a saying in Italy. *Vivi il presente*. It means *to live in the moment*." He picks up his fork and knife and cuts into his steak.

"We have a saying where I'm from too," Milo retorts. "Back the fuck off and find your own girl."

I whack Milo in the chest. "Would you stop? Nothing happened. We're just talking."

Before he can say anything else, the real waiter arrives. He looks at the plate on the table and then at the one he's carrying. "Your meal, sir?"

Mr. Lavin looks down at the steak he's just taken a bite of, his brow wrinkling in confusion.

We all turn at the sound of a commotion. A man across the dining room is pointing at our table and gesticulating wildly.

Milo shrugs. "Yeah, I just grabbed that plate off a random table." He salutes the man across the room and yells, "You could do with less red meat, buddy. Heart disease is a killer!"

Mr. Lavin chokes slightly before spitting the food into a napkin. "Well played, Mr. Hamilton."

I put a hand to my forehead. We're going to end up

getting arrested. That's if no one ends up with food poisoning first.

While the waiter takes the renegade plate away, Mr. Lavin suddenly pats his suit pocket and pulls out his cell phone. The smile on his face disappears and he stands.

"*Mi scusi.* I must take this call."

As soon as he's gone, I turn to Milo. "What the hell are you doing?"

I WATCH Mr. Lavin walk away, confident even under pressure. Not many could be so cool even when confronted by a rival. It's annoying that I admire him so much.

Bastard.

"Are you happy now? We'll be lucky if they don't throw us out of this place." Mya's words are cross, but she doesn't really seem angry that I'm here.

"I'm sorry, was I interrupting? You two seemed awfully cozy." My eyes land on the flower next to her plate.

She flushes. "About that. It's not what you think."

"Are you sure? Because it looks like Mr. Lavin asked you on a date and you showed up to have dinner with him."

"Maybe it is what it looks like," Mya continues hurriedly, "but only because my brain functioning was impaired by too much Chunky Monkey. I thought he wanted to talk about the work we put in."

Oh, that Italian fucker wanted to put some work in, all right. He was planning to give her a naked workout in his hotel room later.

"You really thought he wanted to talk about the campaign?"

She huffs. "It seemed like it. At first. But then he told me what you said to him in Vegas. How you told him to stay away from me."

"Of course I did. Mya, that man wants you. The question is whether *you* want *him*, because if you do, then I'll leave now." I slide closer until we're thigh-to-thigh. "But I want you to ask yourself, will he do the things to you I can do?"

Her breathing quickens, and she shifts in her seat.

"Do you get wet when you think of him?" I continue in a low voice, sliding a hand onto her thigh. The thin fabric of her dress is little barrier as my fingers climb higher.

"No. I only feel that way about you." A soft moan slips from her lips when my finger finds home and presses. Hard. If we weren't sitting down already, she would probably collapse.

"Good. Because I wanted to punch that smug fucker's face the entire time he was sitting here." I edge her panties aside.

"*Oh my god*, Milo! We're in public." She sounds appalled, but she's also not saying no.

I grin wickedly, but my finger slows slightly. "Tell me you won't see him again."

She bites her lip. "I won't see him again. Not like this. But maybe it's best if we don't jump right back in. It only hurt so much because I realized how quickly things were moving. I don't want to get hurt again. Men like you don't settle down. And I'm not expecting anything. You never made any promises."

"Oh, but I did. You just weren't listening." I turn, wishing we were anywhere but this cramped booth. "My body made promises to yours the first time we made love. My lips promised you pleasure every time we kissed."

Her eyes look wounded. "You know what I mean. It was just sex. I knew that going in. It's my fault that I suddenly found myself wanting more."

"I know about wanting more, Mya. I've botched this thing so badly I don't even know where to begin to repair things, so I'll do what I should have done that night in Vegas." I grab her hand. "Mya Christine Taylor, I have been in love with you since, well, since forever."

"You love me?" Mya's eyes fill with tears as she tries to yank her hand back. "You've never said that before."

"All those times I made up stupid excuses to argue with you, I was saying *I love you*. When I dropped everything to rescue you from dry humping random guys in a bar, I was saying *I love you*. From poker nights with your parents, to getting kicked out of my own shower, I told you every day in every way I knew how. I'm sorry I'm not better at this."

Mya kisses me softly. "Actually, you're doing just fine."

I yank her back and our lips meet again, and this time there's nothing soft about it. My mouth slants over hers, taking the kiss so deep and wet that I think we both forget where we are.

Until...

Andre clears his throat and we both turn to look at him. "I apologize, Miss Taylor, but I have to cut this short. My brother who is here visiting the States with me has been in a minor accident. I need to go to the hospital."

"Oh no, I'm so sorry to hear that." Mya tries to stand, but I remain seated, blocking her in the booth. She huffs and shoves all her weight at me which does nothing other than cause her to hurt her own hip.

Andre watches us struggling with amusement. "Even though this dinner has not gone the way I'd hoped, I must admit it has been entertaining. Please, stay and enjoy dinner. I've instructed the manager to put it all on my tab." He inclines his head to both of us. "I'll be in touch soon about the campaign. But in the meantime, if either of you ever needs anything, feel free to call."

We both sit in shock as he strides away.

"Did he just say that he would be in touch about–" Mya turns to me with a look of confusion that mirrors how I feel.

I have to give him credit. He knows how to keep us guessing.

"That motherfucker is enjoying this. He knows he's got us on pins and needles about whether we'll get this job. But I don't even care anymore."

"You don't?"

"No. This account has been nothing but trouble from the start."

"Why didn't you tell me what was going on in Vegas?"

"Because I didn't want to put you in that position. I wasn't sure if you'd feel pressured to flirt with him to get the account. Not that I thought James would ask you to but still, the pressure would have been there."

I hesitate. That's not entirely the truth, but the answer to this question is complicated.

And revealing.

But then I think of everything we've gone through to get to this moment. Most of the trouble could have been avoided if I'd just been honest and hadn't let my fear of rejection steer the way. Mya is nothing like Tessa. She's never done anything to make me believe she cares about power or position.

In fact, the only thing she's ever actually asked me for is... me.

"That was part of it, but also, he's handsome, rich, and well-connected. All I could think was that I'd lose you before I even had the chance to tell you how I feel."

"You were jealous." Her voice trembles slightly.

She's not going to let me off the hook even now. That's my ballbuster.

"Yes, I was jealous."

"You didn't need to be." Mya leans over and kisses my cheek. "I didn't want him. The only man I wanted was the one I was fake engaged to."

Suddenly it hits me that we're still sitting in this restaurant in public when we could be at home. Alone.

"Come on. Let's get out of here."

It's time I prove to Mya that there's nothing fake about my feelings for her. If I want to win her heart, it's time to put it all on the line. These are the highest stakes I've ever encountered, and I'm willing to do whatever it takes to get there.

And I'm not above begging if I have to.

YOU'D THINK after such an intense emotion dump that we'd be super talkative on the way home. But Milo and I are both quiet as we drive back to his place. He keeps looking over at me as if he's afraid that I'll disappear.

Not that I can blame him. I've already pinched myself a time or two.

When we get to his apartment, I drop my bag near the door while he walks around turning on lights. Now that we're alone together, I'm starting to get a little nervous. He said he loves me and that he wants us to be together, but practically speaking, I'm not entirely sure what that means.

Are we going to tell everyone that we're not really engaged but just a couple?

Are we starting over from scratch and going to go on dates?

The thought makes me smile. I can't imagine going to a restaurant to meet Milo for a date like he's just some guy I saw on Tinder.

"I should probably call Ariana. She'll worry if I don't come home."

Milo nods. "We definitely don't want her to worry. She'd show up at the restaurant demanding answers or start an online petition to find out where Mr. Lavin hid your body."

I'm laughing but that's not inaccurate. Ari is a bit of a conspiracy theorist, and if I disappeared for any length of time, she's the type to jump to conclusions.

She answers on the first ring. "Uh oh, if you're calling me that probably means your business deal went bad. Why are you calling me?"

"Everything is fine. Better than fine. Milo showed up and we talked. It turns out that conversation I overheard wasn't about business at all. He was just telling Mr. Lavin that I was already taken."

Ari whistles. "Ooo-kay then. So Happy Hour Hottie was staking his claim. I knew I liked him. I'm really glad he didn't let me down."

"Because it's all about you, huh?"

She snorts. "You're damn straight. No one else had to put up with your grungy ass on the couch eating all the ice cream. So, if you're calling me, that must mean you're with Milo now."

"Yeah. I didn't want you to worry when I didn't come home."

"Now I'm just worried for a different reason."

"What do you mean?"

"Oh, it's nothing. Just tell Triple H that if he gets a bag of exploding dick confetti at work, that I'm sorry."

"*What?*"

"Never mind. Let's let it happen. Consider it future payback for the next time he fucks up. Anyway, have fun!"

I'm still laughing when she hangs up. Exploding dick confetti is probably the tamest on the list of things Ariana could have sent him, so I decide to take her advice and let it happen.

Variety is the spice of life, right?

Our office could use a few surprises.

Milo is in the bedroom and has already changed out of his suit and into sweatpants. His chest is gloriously bare. I sigh. A tiny, shallow part of me is really excited that I get to see this naked chest on a regular basis. Who wouldn't be?

But then I go a little higher and see that warm smile and those wicked eyes, and that's when it hits me how lucky I really am. Because I found love with a guy, who underneath all the suave exterior, is a total sweetheart.

My #boyfriendgoals wish has come true.

"Ariana says hi," I comment as I slip off my shoes and unzip my dress. He's watching me from the bed, and my blood warms under his eyes.

"I want you to move in with me," he whispers.

My heart leaps, and there's a huge part of me that wants to scream *yes, yes, yes,* but I'm not going to abandon everything I've learned lately. This is meant to be, I can feel it, so we don't need to jump into anything. I have a feeling it'll all happen when it's meant to.

I climb on the bed and crawl over to his side. Soon I'm settled into my favorite position, resting on his chest with my ear right over his heart. The heart that I now know beats just for me.

"That might be moving a little fast, but I have to admit that I'm tempted. I do love this bed."

Milo growls playfully and rolls us over until he's on top. "Is that what you love? *My bed?*" His hips nudge mine playfully, teasing a moan from my lips.

"Mmm, hmm. But there *is* something else you can do to convince me." I rub back, enjoying how his eyes narrow when he gets turned on.

"Oh really?"

"Yes. There is one wild, sexy, *kinky* thing that you can do for me."

His tongue is practically hanging out by now.

"What else can I do?" he asks, gazing down at me with his heart in his eyes.

He's so sincere that I almost don't want to fuck with him right now.

But this is Milo. And this is me. So...

I lean up and whisper in his ear, "You can... beg me."

the absolution

MILO

I WON.

Well, not the account. Mya's campaign was chosen. Andre Lavin and the rest of the newly formed Lavin Bridal team were blown away by her concept of a dual vision campaign. From the moment I saw her vision boards, I knew she was going to win. Sometimes you have to know when you've been beaten.

Actually, I'm insanely fucking proud of her. And I got what I wanted in the end after all.

Mya.

It turns out that being vulnerable isn't so painful when your heart is held by someone who cherishes it. After a few more months of dating and a lot of coaxing (and by coaxing, I mean licking her pussy until she agreed), Mya moved into my apartment. She was worried about how Ariana was going to afford the rent, but it turns out she's not the only one with secrets. Ariana has a trust fund big enough for her to afford to live anywhere in the city she wants. She chooses to live modestly.

And she's really fucking happy that we won't be sleeping over anymore so she can stop wearing headphones all the time.

Or at least that's what she said.

I'm not convinced that little perv was actually *ever* wearing the headphones.

There's only one thing that's bothering me lately. Not that it's a *huge* deal, but it's still a deal, you know? Mya and I aren't traditional people, and we don't care about what society dictates is proper or expected. We don't need wedding bands to know how we feel about each other, and a piece of paper won't make me love her any more than I already do.

Because, hello, *not possible*. We're already sky high, baby.

It's just that she's left her laptop open a few times, and I couldn't help noticing she was browsing her old wedding boards on Pinterest. It could be because of the Lavin Bridal campaign, sure.

However, there's still that small chance that she's wishing for the whole deal. After being disappointed so epically once, it's only natural that she'd be a little worried about the concept of forever. Forever used to make me nervous, too. But now it's the only word I can think of when I look at Mya, and I want her to know that.

Plus, she was once planning to marry bad-sex-ex, and like hell if that guy is going to beat me at anything.

Which has me thinking about Vegas.

Mr. Lavin *did* say to call if I ever needed anything.

epilogue

MYA

IT'S BEEN EXACTLY one year since I was last on this same private plane flying to Vegas. That time I was nervous and unsure about where my life was heading. Now I'm in love and getting ready to see the most important campaign of my career up on a billboard. The only thing that hasn't changed–

"OH MY FUCKING GOD, WE'RE ALL GOING TO DIE!"

Milo chuckles and grabs my hand, the one that's not squeezing Chelsea the stress cow. This is our routine whenever we have to fly. I spend the entire time cursing, hyperventilating, and making deals with God about what I'll give up if the plane lands safely, while Milo holds my hand and tries to distract me.

To be honest, just looking at him is usually enough. Especially when he's making those bedroom eyes at me.

He's let his hair grow a little longer at my request, and it falls rakishly around his face. But most importantly, he's happy for me.

I can't believe this is my life.

A few hours later, I wake to find that we've landed. Groggy, I sit up slowly and look around. We weren't the only ones on the flight. Apparently Mr. Lavin had a friend who needed a ride back to the West Coast, too, but the sweet older gentleman who rode with us is gone and so is the flight attendant.

Milo is in the aisle next to me.

Down on one knee.

"Mya, I love you. Every day since you came into my life has been an adventure. An adventure I don't want to end. I know you've been hurt before, planning a wedding that never happened. But I want to assure you there's no way that will happen this time because I want you to marry me today."

"Today?"

He grins. "Yes. Right now, in fact. We can spend the next year planning the perfect wedding, but I don't want to wait another minute for you to be my wife."

He pulls a box from his pocket and flips it open. A beautiful antique gold ring is revealed.

"My mom sent me this not long after I told her about you. It was my grandmother's ring."

With shaky fingers, I stretch out my left hand. He slides the ring on my third finger, and it goes on like it was made for me.

Kind of like the man.

Somehow, he knew my unspoken fear of planning another wedding that might not happen. Now he's made sure my worst fear is impossible because I'll be planning a wedding to the man who is already my husband.

As always, he's three steps ahead looking out for me.

Unlike when he first asked me to move in, I don't bother trying to play it cool. I launch myself into the aisle, bowling us both over in the process.

"*Yes! Yes! Yes!* I can't wait to be your wife. I love you so much."

He wraps an arm around my waist. "I love you, too. Everything has really come full circle hasn't it?"

I look around. "Just a year ago, could you have predicted that we'd be back here? In love and engaged, for real this time. Are you sure you're ready for this?"

"No, but that's the fun, isn't it? Whatever comes, we'll deal with it together." Milo is, as usual, completely confident and absolutely the love of my life.

#husbandgoals

epilogue

MILO

YOU THOUGHT THAT WAS IT?

Hell no. Because my lady deserves a lot more than just a Vegas wedding. She deserves the whole shebang. Especially the bang.

Okay come on, you wouldn't be able to resist that one either.

My completely bangable wife walks in and everything else fades to gray. We've been married about six months now, and I don't think I'll ever get tired of saying that. *My wife.* The woman who has taught me that there's not a damn thing wrong with slowing things down sometimes, and who continues to keep me on my toes with her sharp tongue. I'm quite a fan of what she can do with that tongue, actually.

"I can't believe today is the day!" She's radiating happiness.

"I'm glad your whole family could make it. I know they were really disappointed that we eloped. Now bring your sexy ass over here and help me eat the rest of this food."

It's the morning of our wedding, well, our second wedding, and we've been lounging in bed all morning, dividing our attention between breakfast and each other.

She climbs on the bed and I cut off a small bit of a waffle and hold it out to her. "Open up."

I watch with heated eyes as the tines of the fork slide between her lips.

"You're staring." She chews slowly, flushing as my eyes follow the movement.

"I can't help it. I love watching you eat." I polish off the rest of the food and set the tray on the table next to the bed.

"Really?"

Mya licks a bit of syrup from the edge of her mouth. She looks bewildered. Then again, she has no idea how much time I spend imagining those lips wrapped around my cock.

"You have a mouth made for sin. Breakfast meetings with you were always torture."

"Milo! I would have never guessed. You always seemed so... focused."

"I was focusing all right. Just not on what I should have been." I grin as she ducks her head.

Blushing, she reaches over and snags a doughnut off the tray on the bedside table. "I suppose I shouldn't be so shocked since I used to do the same thing. In fact..." She traces a finger around the hole and peeks up at me. When our eyes meet, she glances away quickly.

"What? What are you thinking?" My heart speeds up as she tilts her head to the side, like a naughty angel with her pouty lips and her innocent expression.

"Mya," I say warningly as she climbs over my legs. The edges of her lips pull up into a hint of a smile, and then she disappears beneath the covers.

Damn. I have a feeling she's about to show me a new meaning of torture. Especially since it hasn't escaped my notice that she took the doughnut with her.

A sticky hand wraps around my cock, and I jump at the contact. A soft giggle floats up from under the covers. I move back to make space for her between my legs.

Is she really going to?

My silent prayer is answered a second later when I feel the soft dough roll over the length of my cock.

My head falls back onto the pillow as I absorb the sensation of the soft pastry moving over my skin. Her hot, wet mouth follows, her tongue licking and nipping every inch of my length as it rolls through the doughnut. Soft curls flow over my legs and belly, teasing me with trailing fingers of sensation.

I tug the covers down until I can see her, and the drool-worthy scene of Mya on her knees loving me with her mouth is something I'll never forget.

No one has ever taken such time to savor me, to figure out what drives me crazy. It gives me an absurd sense of pride to see my woman taking such pleasure in my response.

My woman.

My wife.

Pleasure sweeps through me, waves of sensation tingling over every inch of my skin. My fingers tangle in the sheets as she manages to take me all the way to the root, hollowing her cheeks as she sucks.

"Holy. Shit." The rasp of my voice betrays my emotions. I'm holding on by only a fine thread of control. "We're definitely going to be late."

She laughs huskily, the sound of a woman who knows exactly what she's doing. I watch helplessly as she wets the tip of her finger and circles the head of my dick.

"Wait," I rasp, unsure what she's doing now, only that I'll die if she stops.

"Don't worry. I'm not going anywhere." She licks my skin right above the doughnut. "I haven't finished my breakfast yet."

I tangle my fingers in her hair as her mouth finally takes me back in. She sucks and licks around my length before taking a small nibble of the doughnut. She alternates between sucking my cock and nipping at the pastry until I think I might die from the fire racing up my spine.

Finally, there is only a small bit of the doughnut left, and she scoops it up and pops it in her mouth. I wait, poised on the edge of madness, until she returns and licks every last bit of sticky sugar from my skin.

"That's it." I sit up and roll her onto her back. Her soft *oh* of surprise is swallowed by my kiss as her hands snake around my back to grip my ass. Her legs wrap around me as I sink into the valley between her thighs, her hips cradling me as if I were coming home.

"God, I love you."

The words aren't enough, completely inadequate to describe how she's changed my life. But somehow, she seems to know what I mean. She always seems to know.

"I feel it when you look at me," she whispers. She runs a hand gently through my hair. "I feel desirable and smart, strong and sexy. All the things I've always wanted to be."

"You *are* all those things. You're amazing. And all mine."

I thrust my tongue into her mouth while my hands stroke all over her skin. Her nipples peak, and my fingers find the stiff tips as if they heard them cry out for my attention.

"That feels amazing. Everything with you is amazing." She closes her eyes at the intimate touch.

I drop my forehead to hers, looking deeply into her eyes as I push inside. She looks down, riveted by the sight of my cock gliding in and out. It's so erotic to watch us together.

Tension builds with each of my movements until she's strung tight as a bowstring. Every touch of my hands, every thrust, takes her higher until I'm sure we're both on the verge of breaking apart. This is what I always want. Her pleasure and my pleasure together.

I fit my hands under her hips, holding her captive. "Come with me."

And just like everything else, she gives it all to me.

———

IT'S NOT my fault that we're almost late to our own wedding.

Not entirely, anyway.

Ethan snickers when we finally stumble through the doors of the church.

"You're in trouble," he mutters as we hustle down the hallway to the rooms where we're supposed to change.

"What the hell were you guys doing?" Ariana asks. Then she wrinkles her nose at my knowing grin. "You guys have been married for ages. You couldn't bone when we're not on a schedule?"

The girls disappear, leaving Ethan and I to do what guys have done before weddings for time immemorial.

Wait.

"Glad you bothered to show up to your own wedding, bro. That Ariana chick was pissed. And she is scary. Scary hot, though." Ethan looks behind us at the door. "Maybe it's time I get back out there. You make the old ball and chain look good."

"Whoa, proceed with caution. It's been a year and I'm still finding wang-shaped confetti in my ears."

Ethan cracks up. "The fact that I actually understood that sentence concerns me. I always did like them feisty."

Ariana's voice pipes up from the doorway. "Feisty is for Chihuahuas and bad Thai food."

Busted.

We both turn around slowly. Ethan is grinning at her in a way that says he plans on trying to take her on anyway, which should be interesting. Possibly dangerous, but definitely interesting.

"Mya is ready now."

That's all I need to hear. I leave them talking and head for the room next door.

We're already married, so we didn't see the point of keeping the whole *don't see the bride before the wedding* superstitions, because, yeah, I wasn't doing that. But Mya did say that she wanted to surprise me with her dress.

And when I open the door, I'm not just surprised. I'm humbled.

She's the most beautiful thing I've ever seen.

"You are stunning," I say, once I've caught my breath.

Mya clutches her bouquet with trembling fingers. Her dress is strapless and fits close, hugging her curves lovingly before flaring out behind her in a modest train. She skipped the veil and opted for a sparkling tiara instead. Her usual braid has been replaced with a loose bun adorned with tiny white flowers.

"You look pretty dapper yourself."

We share a grin. Her dress is her mother's, modified and redesigned to fit Mya, but my suit is from the upcoming Lavin Bridal launch.

What? I look damn good in it, too.

"Thank you for being such a good sport about this." Mya strokes my collar into place. "You probably think it's silly having a wedding when you're already married."

"If you want a wedding, you get a wedding." I kiss her nose gently so I won't ruin her makeup.

The small anteroom of the church isn't exactly soundproof, so I can hear the clamor of voices and the soft music provided by the harpist. Everything has been planned by Mya down to the finest detail. We'll have a short ceremony followed by a catered reception.

None of it really matters to me, let's be real, but I care that it matters to *her*.

My life's mission is to give her everything she wants.

It might seem indulgent to others that we're having another wedding, but when have I ever given a shit what anyone thinks? This is our time to celebrate with the people who love us. Mya's parents and my mom and brother have met, of course, but for the first time, our extended families will be able to meet and mingle.

The beginning of forging a new family. One strong enough to last a lifetime.

The door opens, and Ariana sticks her head in. "Five minutes, guys."

Once the door closes behind her, I resume my place behind Mya, nuzzling her neck. Suddenly I'm really glad we went non-traditional. Since we're already married, I don't have to wait at the front of the aisle while Mya's parents give her away.

I've already got her, and I'm never giving her back. My hands curve around her waist.

"Don't you dare start something right before we have to walk down the aisle!" She squirms playfully, but when I start to move away, she makes this sexy little noise and pushes her lace-clad bottom against me.

Instant. Boner.

I think I've discovered a new fetish. Mya in a wedding dress is my new favorite fantasy.

"Yes, Mrs. Taylor-Hamilton. I'm on my best behavior."

Mya turns her head and nuzzles me right back. "Yeah right. But I love your bad behavior. Except in front of my parents. If you mention *anything* about our sex bet in front of my parents, I will kill you."

My lips pull up into a dirty grin. "Come on, admit it. I did have you begging."

"You're still trying to get me to admit you won that bet, huh?"

"Can you blame me? I love winning."

Her fingers slide into my hair. "You can't win something that's already yours. And I am, Milo. I've been yours all along."

Well what do you know?

I didn't think anything could be more satisfying than winning. Or hearing her beg me for more.

But it turns out I love hearing her pledge her heart to me best of all.

———

I hope you enjoyed BEG ME!

WANT MORE? After a certain person (*ahem Milo*) had a little too much fun at Happy Hour, HR sent out a memo about appropriate behavior. Join my newsletter at mmalonebooks.com to get your free bonus scene *About That Happy Hour*!

———

Are you a fan of small town gossip and grumpy heroes? If so, you'll love *You Ruin Everything*! It's pure romantic comedy with a zany family, a pug with a vendetta and a heroine you can root for!

SWINGING a hammer does not make up for being grumpy and shirtless all the time. But Hendrix Evers thinks renovating my Gran's run-down Victorian is the perfect reason to let him move in. Everyone thinks he's this hardworking, small town hero, but he's my best friend's brother so I know the truth. He's rude, juvenile and has a long history of ruining things for me. But surely we can co-exist for one summer without bloodshed, right? **Start reading now!**

———

Are you ready for more office romance shenanigans? I hope so because Andre Lavin is back in town in the next book, ASK ME!

If it's possible to screw up a good thing, I'm the girl who'll figure out how. So when I get a new job, I celebrate with one last night of fun before focusing on climbing the corporate ladder. Until my night of fun walks into the office and I discover who he really is. **Start reading ASK ME now!**

Turn the page to read an exclusive excerpt. Although I have to warn you, these books are best avoided if you are in any danger of peeing when you laugh. Just... trust me.

DING DONG I JUST GOT DITCHED

Andre

I'm *that* guy. The one women want and other men want *to be.*

Arrogant? Maybe. Accurate? Abso-F'ing-lutely.

So when my brother dares me to hit on women as a regular guy, I'm up for the challenge. It turns out quite a few ladies like ripped jeans just as much as haute couture. Except for one. Casey. Nothing I do impresses this girl which only makes me want her more. For the first time, I'm smitten.

Until she ditches me after a night of intense passion.

Casey

If it's possible to screw up a good thing, I'm the girl who'll figure out how. So when I get a new job, I celebrate with one last night of fun before focusing on climbing the corporate ladder.

Until my night of fun walks into the office and I discover who he really is. My firm's biggest client and my new nightmare.

Egotistical, entitled and infuriating, Andre Lavin is not making it easy for me to ignore him. In a battle of wills, we'll see who can hold out the longest.

And who is still standing at the end.

ASK ME is the kind of outrageous romantic comedy that will have you clutching your pearls and laughing until you cry! This standalone romance features crossover characters from the USA TODAY bestselling book BEG ME.

Get ASK ME Now

at minxmalone.com/askme

Excerpt of ASK ME © M. Malone

ANDRE

Something tickles my nose and I open my eyes. Sunlight streams through the curtains I forgot to close last night. Drapes were definitely the last thing on my mind when we stumbled into this room.

I blink sleepily and peer around the unfamiliar room. Kate is a miracle worker. Seriously, best assistant ever. Who else could I call and ask for a new hotel room and have the digital key on my app less than ten minutes later? Amazing.

Not sure what miracle she pulled off to have a room ready for me that fast but I don't care. All I care about is the results. There was no way I could bring Casey up to the Presidential Suite after spending so much effort to get her to see me as a regular guy.

And she did. She knows nothing of what I do for a living or about the money or the fame. To her, I'm just a guy with slightly bad fashion sense who seems to bump into her a lot. And yet, she likes me anyway.

My chest warms when I think about her and that's when it hits me. My head whips to the right, the space where Casey should be.

The space that contains nothing but rumpled sheets and a pillow.

Suddenly wide awake, I sit straight up and kick the

blanket off. I'm still naked but I don't care about that as I walk over to the bathroom and knock on the door. When I open it, it's empty. Heart pumping now, I run to the door of the room and step out into the hall.

"Oh my!"

There's a middle-aged couple in the hall pushing a baby in a stroller. The mother covers her mouth in surprise but her eyes drop to my dick swinging in the wind. The father scowls at me and then puts his hand over his wife's eyes.

"Sorry." I close the door and lean back against it. There's no way around it.

Casey left.

Perplexed, I stalk around the room staring at the rumpled bed linens as if they can give me the answers. Did I do something to scare her away? It's not bragging to say that I've never had a woman run out on me before. Usually, morning afters consist of round four or five of sex followed by a leisurely brunch.

Then I'm usually the one trying to find a tactful way to escape.

But this ... I don't know what to make of this. She ditched me! The more I think about it, the more absurd it seems. As I'm pacing, my foot runs over something and I lean down to pick it up. My blood heats when I see what it is. The panties I peeled off Casey last night.

I chuckle, only now able to see the design on the cotton.

Purple and pink unicorns cover the fabric. As pissed off as I am, I can't help laughing. Only Casey could wear such unsexy panties and still have me panting for more. Maybe it's a metaphor for this whole situation. She's like this mythical creature that I've only dreamed up. Hell, maybe I had one too many beers last night and the whole thing was a dream.

Then I'm hit with a visceral memory of her tight, wet heat as I slid inside her, the way she moaned in my ear and shuddered beneath me every time she came.

That wasn't a dream. It was the best damn sex I've ever had. And instead of enjoying more of it, I'm standing in the middle of a basic hotel room with a stiff dick holding the most ridiculous panties I've ever seen.

My phone is still on the nightstand where I put it last night. I'm checking for messages when it hits me. We never exchanged numbers. I don't even think I got her last name. I look over at her side of the bed again and that's when I see the note propped up on the other nightstand. I crawl over the bed and snatch it eagerly. It's just two lines scrawled on the hotel stationery.

Last night was amazing.

You really are my lucky charm.

I stare at the paper in disbelief. That's it? Just two lines and she didn't even sign her name?

Then I see that she's written something on the outside.

When I peer closer what I see scrawled there only makes me feel worse.

No, what I see written there makes my blood boil.

"Who the fuck is *Andrew*?"

Get ASK ME Now

at minxmalone.com/askme

BEATRICE

Thinking about trying a dating app? My advice- *don't.* Seriously, save yourself.

If I wasn't on a dating app, I never would have been hiding in the bathroom of an Italian restaurant to avoid the most aggressive of Crypto Bros. And I never would have called the one person who *always* bails me out. August Gordon.

Once upon a time he was the adorkable guy who helped me with my biology homework. Now he is six-foot one with eyes like a dream. Now he's the guy who kissed me on the forehead before saying something that made Crypto Bro look scared for his life.

Nope. This is not happening.

I am not falling for my best friend. Because things between us have always been easy. Uncomplicated.

But if there's one thing I'm good at, it's complicating things.

BEATRICE

I can't let him come outside with me. I already told him I called an Uber so I don't want him to see Auggie waiting for me.

And I *definitely* don't want Auggie to see him.

It's not like we haven't talked about dating before but something about Auggie actually seeing me on a date feels weird. Luca seemed good-looking on his profile, but standing next to August, I'm pretty sure he'll look like a pale imitation of what a man should be.

Actually seeing Auggie is pretty much a guarantee to kill any date, even if the guy isn't glued to his phone.

"You should go ahead," I continue. "It was nice meeting you, Luca."

But his grip only tightens, his voice holding a trace of annoyance as he says, "You're not going to let me see you home, Bea? You already spent half the time in the bathroom and now you're leaving early? That's just rude."

I pull back, trying to yank my arm free. "What?"

His aggression is startling, an unwelcome shift from the apathetic facade he displayed earlier. I figured he'd be a little disappointed but not this upset. Then again, nothing about this date has been what I imagined it would be.

"You're one of those women who just use men. You just wanted a free dinner and now you're trying to ditch me," he snaps.

His words echo in my head. Yes, I was trying to ditch him, but not for the reasons he thought.

"Um, I paid for my half of dinner. So…"

I wasn't going to message him again anyway but after this sudden show of aggression, I no longer feel even slightly bad about that decision. Now I just need to get away. But before I can respond, or turn to walk away, I see a familiar figure come through the door of the restaurant.

August.

He takes in my stance next to the booth and Luca's hand on my arm with a darkening scowl. Luca follows my gaze to see what I'm looking at and he glances at me uncertainly as August heads our way.

"You're going to want to let go of her arm now," Auggie growls.

"Who are you?" Luca asks.

Instead of answering, Auggie steps closer until he's right up in Luca's face. The move breaks his hold on my arm, thankfully and I rub the spot which is already getting sore. Auggie sweeps his arm around, folding me close against his back and out of Luca's sight.

"Don't look at her," Auggie barks when Luca tries to look around him at me. "Talk to me."

"I don't even know you," Luca mutters.

"Exactly. And you don't know her either. From this moment on, you have permanent amnesia when it comes to her. Got it?"

"Wait a minute. You can't just–"

Auggie turns around, completely ignoring my blustering date behind him. His lips against my forehead shock me out of the trance I've been in since he showed up.

"Go wait for me right outside, okay?" Auggie says in a low voice.

"Okay," I mumble, not entirely sure what's going on but happy to get away.

Auggie watches me as I walk to the door of the restaurant. Once I push through, he turns back to Luca. There is a large party coming in at the same time as I'm leaving so I step aside to let them through. Once it's clear, I step back up to the window to look back in. The guys are still talking but all I can see are their profiles. Auggie seems to tower over Luca, and with every word the other man seems to shrink. As Auggie continues to speak, Luca's shoulders hunch, his earlier bravado crumbling under August's intensity.

Finally August steps away and when he turns, his face is completely blank. Our eyes meet through the window and the air buzzes with something electric. Caught, I quickly step back and stare aimlessly at the cars going by. My heart is racing for some reason I can't identify.

What was that? I wouldn't have believed it if I hadn't seen it myself. My aggressive date had been completely shut down by whatever Auggie said.

And I am completely turned on.

Join the fun at patreon.com/minxmalone

Ask Me : Am I arrogant? Maybe. Do women still want me? Abso-F'ing-lutely. Then I meet the one woman who isn't impressed.

Want Me : No strings attached. Sounds good, right? Except if I'm not her boyfriend ... the position is open for someone else.

Need Me : Crazy sh*t every day keeps relationships away. Except there's one guy who just *keeps* showing up. And if I'm not careful, I might get used to needing someone.

BLUE-COLLAR BILLIONAIRES

Inheriting billions from the father they never knew sounds like a pretty sweet deal. Until they find out what he really wants in exchange.

Tank : Fake Dating the billionaire's son should have been easy. He's a bad boy and not my type. But he's also loyal and kind with an unexpected soft spot for rescue cats. Suddenly all I want is for this "fake" love to be real.

Finn : When she left me, I had nothing. Now I have it all: money, cars and most importantly, power. She's struggling to save her business, and I'm in the perfect position to save it. For a price.

Gabe : She thinks I'm arrogant and cocky as hell. She's right. A reformed con artist and a perfect little princess don't belong together. But I still can't leave her alone.

Zack : She's my brother's ex. Off limits. But she needs a nude model for her show so I'm taking one for the team. Turns out she needs more than just my picture...

Luke : My online BFF is the only hacker better than I am. Then

I'm asked to consult on a hacking case for the FBI and the hauntingly beautiful suspect seems to know a lot about me. Things I've only told one other person...

Blue-Collar Christmas : Emma has a plan to bring the high-rolling billionaire Marshall brothers back to their roots with the perfect blue-collar Christmas. But it turns out the "perfect" Christmas has a price tag no one expected...

BAD BUSINESS

(The Kingsleys)

Bad King: My parents just put a gold diggers target on my back. But if all they want is a wedding, I'll find the fiancee of their nightmares. *Who Wants to Marry a Billionaire? Must be completely inappropriate.*

Bad Blood : I'd do anything for my best friend's little sister. Until she asks for the one thing I can't give. One night. No rules. ***RITA® Award Winner!***

THE ALEXANDERS

One More Day : "Good girl" Ridley has always attracted bad guys. Now she's on the run and has nowhere to hide. So when Jackson Alexander mistakes her for her twin, she decides to do something she knows is wrong. *She lies.*

The Things I Do for You : Nick Alexander finally has what the woman of his dreams needs. He'll give Raina a baby if she gives him what he wants. *Her*.

All I Want: All Kaylee wants is for Elliott Alexander to notice she's alive. When her car skids out of control on Christmas Eve, she's forced to reach out to the only man she trusts to save her. **(VIP List only)**

All I Need is You : When the man she loves leaves town after their steamy kiss, Kaylee Wilhelm is done. But when she's targeted by a stalker, Eli is the only one who can protect her.

Just One Thing : Bennett Alexander is a bona fide genius but he still can't figure out how to "get the girl". So he hires a dating tutor. What could go wrong? Other than falling for his teacher, of course.

One More Chance : Now that Ridley is expecting, everything is different. All she needs is for Jackson to pretend that he finds her as sexy as he used to, even if it's not true. But with a little advice from her meddlesome twin, she has a plan to seduce her own husband.

THE SIMMONS

Birthday Cake : Ever since Mara walked into her brother's dorm room freshman year and came face to face with a shirtless Trent, she's known he was *The One*. She finally has a plan to get him exactly where she wants him. *In her bed*.

He's the Man : Matt Simmons is over Army doctors poking him until he sees his old babysitter, now a physical therapist, is h-o-t. Suddenly he's seeing the benefits of therapy.

Say You Will : Mara Simmons has always known Trent Townsend is *The One*. But when she suspects his frequent business trips have *nothing* to do with business, she sets in motion a chain of events bigger than she can imagine and discovers that the man she loves just might be a stranger.

Join my VIP list for FREE books

newsletter.mmalonebooks.com

about the author

M. Malone is a RITA® Award winner and a NYT & USA Today Bestselling author of completely inappropriate romantic comedy. She lives with her husband and their two sons in the picturesque mountains of Northern Virginia even though she is afraid of insects, birds, butterflies and other humans.

She also holds a Master's degree in Business from a prestigious college that would no doubt be scandalized at how she's using her expensive education.

mmalonebooks.com